FROZEN FISH FINGERS

JASON BERESFORD

ILLUSTRATED BY Vicky Barker

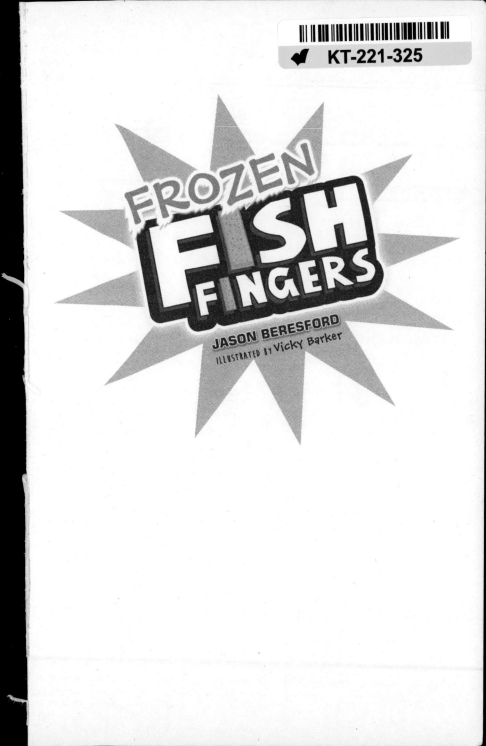

FROZEN FISH FINGERS

JASON BERESFORD

ILLUSTRATED BY Vicky Barker

Catnip

CATNIP BOOKS
Published by Catnip Publishing Ltd
320 City Road
London
EC1V 2NZ

This edition first published 2014

3 5 7 9 10 8 6 4

A CIP catalogue record for this book is available from the British Library.

ISBN 978-1-84647-1834

Printed and bound by CPI Group (UK) Ltd, Croydon, CR0 4YY
www.lfbookservices.co.uk

www.catnippublishing.co.uk

To my little brother Andy, all 6'2" of him.

GARY, BEL, RUBY AND MORRIS
USED TO BE ORDINARY KIDS, LIVING ORDINARY LIVES ON FISH STREET. . .

The only extraordinary thing about them was the extraordinary number of donuts Morris could eat without getting a tummy ache.

But then they met an elf.
And that elf turned them into
SECRET SUPERHEROES.

Now in times of trouble,
Gary Gamble becomes ***THE CHIMP***, with the springy agility of a chimpanzee.
Bel Singh, AKA ***NIGHTINGALE***, flies and sings with a voice so powerful it shakes the trees.
Ruby Rudd is ***KANGARUBY***, who bounces like a kangaroo and has a magic pocket.
And Morris Tweddle becomes ***SLUG BOY*** who . . . er, shrinks to the size of a sausage and wobbles about a bit.
They've vowed to help:

WHOEVER THEY CAN,
WHEREVER THEY CAN,
WHENEVER THEY CAN.

(Unless it's getting a bit late because they might have to go home for their tea.)
Their superpowers only last for ***an hour*** but when the four friends come to the rescue they are totally fabulous.

In Fact, they are . . .

THE FABULOUS FOUR FISH FINGERS

PRELUDE…

BLAST FROM THE PAST

Crouching inside a tunnel in the depths of Castle Gristle, Dr Ernest Grubski was sawing through an ancient pipe. Grubski was Transyldovia's maddest scientist. His eyes were goggly, his teeth were missing and his hair grew like the roots of a spring onion. He was never going to win Transyldovia's Mr Drop Dead Gorgeous competition, but he was clever. Dangerously clever. He was the kind of scientist who could put lightning in a jam jar, or make a bomb out of cheese or think of fifty-seven ways to kill a slug (all of them squishy and revolting).

Grubski didn't like being in the tunnels – he much preferred his lab – but he was determined to answer a question that had been troubling him for months: *Why did the toilet in his en-suite bathroom keep flooding?* Grubski had followed the pipework to this spot and figured it must be the source of the blockage. He gave the saw an extra heave-ho and the pipe split apart, spilling filthy water over his shoes.

'**Yuuuggghh**,' groaned the scientist but then

something else dropped out of the pipework. Grubski caught it and held it up to the light.

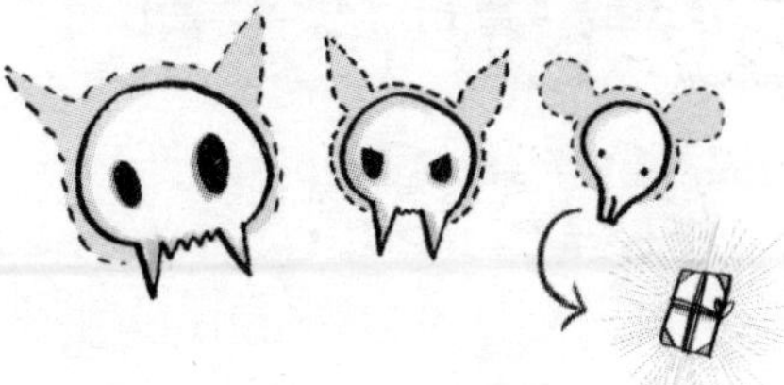

It was the skull of a cat.

Inside was the skull of a bat.

Inside that was the skull of a rat.

Inside that was a tiny book, wrapped in wax paper, inscribed with the name *Vladi the Baddie.*

It was a good job Grubski could do basic plumbing or he'd never have found it.

The scientist's blood raced. He knew immediately that he was staring at a priceless treasure. 'I've found the unholy grail!' he whispered. He'd heard rumours about Vladi's diary for years, but never dreamed he would hold it in his hands. Three centuries before, Vladi the Baddie had ruled Transyldovia with an iron fist, a black heart and pointy teeth. He was cruel and bloodthirsty. Some said he was a wizard. Others claimed he was a vampire. A few said he was a Sagittarius. Whatever the truth, Grubski felt sure this book would teach him the secrets of Vladi's power.

Grubski dashed back to the lab, switched on a

reading lamp and settled into a chair, anxious to read the diary in peace. He was about to open the book when his computer beep-beep-beeped. A robotic voice said, 'This is a reminder. Fix the toilet. Follow the pipework. Locate the blockage . . .'

'I've already done it,' said Grubski, getting up to turn the computer off. It seemed to be stuck.

'This is a reminder. Fix the toilet. . .'

'I said I've done it!' snapped Grubski, pressing the keypad.

'. . . follow the pipework. Locate . . .'

'**SHUUUUUUT UPP!**' yelled Grubski, yanking out the plug.

'No need to be nasty,' said the machine. 'I was only saying, fix the toilet, follow the pipework, locate . . .'

Grubski grabbed the hammer he kept for emergencies and bashed the computer as hard as he could. It didn't remind him of anything after that. Although it did mutter something about 'unreasonable working conditions' whenever he was in earshot.

Grubski hurried back to his chair and was just getting comfy when he was interrupted again. A screechy version of the Transyldovian national anthem (*Transyldovia, There's Snow All Over Ya*) sang out from his pocket. His evil twin, who was even more evil than Grubski, was ringing his mobile.

Grubski fumbled for the answer button.

'Have you fixed the bathroom yet?' asked his twin.

'I'm busy at the moment,' said Grubski.

'You've been saying that for months. Do it now!'

'If you must know I . . .' But Grubski's twin had already hung up.

The doctor scowled, turned his phone off and shoved it under a cushion for good measure. *Peace at last,* he thought as he opened the book. Then his landline rang. He'd forgotten he even had one. Twitching like a man with porcupines in his pyjamas, Grubski stomped across the room and snatched up the receiver. '**WHAT!**' he yelled.

A cheerful girl said, 'Hello! Have you thought about switching your electricity supplier? We have great deals on gas too! Windows, car . . . '

'**YAAAAAAAAAAGGGGGGGGGGGGHHHHHHHH!**' screamed the doctor, using his emergency hammer again.

The scientist counted to ten, then, finally, he started to read the diary. Written in Vladi's own hand, it contained the details of innocent people he'd tortured, enemies he'd bumped off and even a few recipes. There was also an old sock in between two pages that he must have used as a bookmark. And then, on the last page, Grubski spotted something very, very interesting. It was a prophecy. His eyes grew even gogglier as he read the first lines:

300 years from my jubilee
Sniff out a vampire under a treee
Get a class of kids from over the foam . . .

He laughed as he examined the rest of the prophecy. '**HE CAN'T SPELL TREE BUT APART FROM THAT, THE MAN WAS A GENIUS!**' Grubski shouted out loud. 'This prophecy is the key to everlasting power in Transyldovia. I only have to follow Vladi's instructions and the presidential palace will be mine forever. Okay, make that *ours* forever.' He was thinking of his even more evil twin. 'Two Grubskis are better than one I suppose. Let's see, 300 years from Vladi's jubilee. That'll be in about ***six years, four months, three weeks and four days***.'

Nearly six years, four months, three weeks and four days later . . .

YULE BE SORRY

It was only the beginning of December, but the queue still stretched right down Fish Street to the old supermarket car park, where a shed decked with fairy lights was standing in a forest of plastic trees and fake snow.

Shivering under a sign that read *Santa's Grotto*, little Lucy Cotton was next to go in.

'It's so exciting!' she whispered to her grandad, who held her tightly by the hand.

'Not long now, Luce,' said her grandad.

A voice shouted, '**NEXT!**' and the Cottons stepped inside, ready to gasp in amazement . . .

Instead, they found the grottiest grotto they'd ever seen. Tatty tinsel hung from the ceiling, a Christmas tree with no branches drooped in a bucket and a fat cat in plastic antlers was snoring on the back seat of a sleigh.

'Merry, er, thingy,' growled a man who looked like Santa, but smelled like those slimy green things everyone throws out of their hamburgers.

The Cottons had stumbled into the lair of Father Xxxmas, the fake Santa with maggots in his beard.

'Hello, Santa,' said Lucy brightly, not realising she was face to face with one of Tumchester's nastiest supervillains.

'I ain't got time to listen to your wish list,' said Father Xxxmas. 'Send me a text or an email or something. Take a present from the sack and off you go.'

He stood up and a shower of maggots dropped from his beard on to the floor. Lucy thought they must be snowflakes.

Then Father Xxxmas shook Lucy's grandad by the hand. 'You'll find a maze out the back. Kids love it. Merry – you know, whatever it is,' and he shoved both his visitors though the back door.

'**NOW LOOK HERE!**' shouted Lucy's grandad, but the door was now locked and outside they found dozens of other dissatisfied customers, searching for the exit in the plastic trees.

'Santa wasn't as nice as I thought he'd be,' said Lucy. 'But at least I got a present.' Excitedly she unwrapped her parcel . . . only to find a box of toenail clippings. As Lucy began to cry, a boy came over.

'You were lucky,' he said. 'I got a dead fly. And

my brother got a snotty tissue full of bogies.'

Another girl said, 'I got some rabbit droppings. Santa must be running out of toys. And magic.'

While the grown-ups tried to comfort their sobbing children, Father Xxxmas chuckled to himself and checked his new watch. (He'd stolen it from Lucy's grandad when they shook hands).

'Looks like it's time to go!' he sniggered.

Then he tossed the watch into a huge sack full of wedding rings, necklaces, earrings, mobile phones and wallets that he'd also pilfered that day. He gave the maggots in his beard a tickle and climbed into his sleigh.

Father Xxxmas's sleigh was the only thing about him that wasn't cheap and nasty. Instead of being pulled by reindeer, it had a flying motorbike on the front and it was speedier than Tumchester's fastest police car.

Xxxmas was just putting his crash helmet on when the grotto door swung open.

In stepped The Chimp, Nightingale, KangaRuby and Slug Boy. To be honest, Slug Boy didn't do any stepping – the others did that since they had all the legs. Slug Boy just sat squelchily in the clear, plastic Slugmobile that hung from Nightingale's wrist.

'Season's greetings,' said The Chimp. 'We are The Fabulous Four Fish Fingers. And you are a Christmas turkey who's about to get stuffed.'

'The only prezzie you'll get this year is a prison uniform,' said KangaRuby.

'But I think the colour might suit you,' said Nightingale.

'It's grey,' added Slug Boy. 'A nice change from that red number you always wear.'

'**HO-HO-HOPELESS!**' scoffed the villain. 'I don't need fashion tips from pipsqueaks in purple tracksuits. Or a talking poo-in-a-box.'

'That's disgusting!' spluttered Slug Boy. 'It's not a box. It's a Slugmobile.'

'Whatever. See you next Christmas,' said Father Xxxmas, revving up his sleigh. As smoke billowed from the exhaust pipes he began to blast off, but The Chimp somersaulted across the floor and grabbed him by the beard.

'**YEEEOOOOW!!! GEEERRRRRROOFFFFF**,' screamed Father Xxxmas. '**YOU'RE UPSETTING MY MAGGGGGGGOTS!**'

KangaRuby was quick to follow The Chimp's lead. Her fingers were a blur as she dipped into her magic pocket and started pulling out things

to throw. First she hit Father Xxxmas with a tennis racquet. Then a flip-flop, two onions and an ironing board. It was the ironing board that knocked him off the sleigh and sent all his maggots scurrying to his armpits for some peace and quiet.

The villain lay groggily on the grotto floor. 'Rudolph! Help!!!' he yelled.

The mangy cat in antlers sprang up from the back of the sleigh and clamped its mouth shut on The Chimp's ankle like a Venus flytrap round a bluebottle. Now it was The Chimp's turn to yell.

'AAAAAAGGGGGHHHHHHHHH!!!'

Xxxmas seized his chance. He jumped back on the sleigh and twisted the throttle. His mangy cat leapt aboard and Xxxmas rocketed through the roof, leaving a cloud of splinters.

'IF YOU THINK YOU CAN STOP ME, YOU'RE CHRISTMAS CRACKERS!' shouted the crook, disappearing into the clouds.

The Fish Fingers weren't beaten yet, though. Nightingale soared into the air, Slug Boy in the Slugmobile dangling from her wrist.

'**HERE, TAKE THIS!**' KangaRuby shouted after her and she threw the tennis racquet up to Nightingale, who caught it with one hand.

As Nightingale shot skywards, she turned to Slug Boy. 'Right, what do you think?'

'I think I'm going to chuck up my breakfast,' he replied. Slug Boy always got travel sick when Nightingale flew this fast.

'Hang in there,' she said, giving her arms an extra fast flap. 'I've spotted him.'

As Nightingale closed in, Father Xxxmas saw her in his mirror. He swerved quickly to shake her off and she vanished into a thick bank of cloud. Father Xxxmas couldn't believe his luck. '***Must've got lost!***' he laughed. '***Ho ho ho!***'

Hidden in the cloud cover, Nightingale flipped open the Slugmobile and flicked Slug Boy into the air. Aiming carefully, she whacked him with the tennis racquet and the little superhero flew like a ball served at Wimbledon. He could definitely taste his breakfast now (custard donuts, jam donuts, chocolate donuts and a plate of pilchards. His mum wasn't much of a cook). Slug Boy flew, eyes

outstretched, skin wobbling, lips wibbling, cheeks flapping, before hitting his target – the exhaust pipe on Father Xxxmas's sleigh – perfectly. He wedged himself inside.

Xxxmas couldn't figure out what was wrong as his engine began to splutter and wheeze. He twisted the throttle, banged the handlebars and frantically turned the key, but it didn't make any difference. The engine rattled for a few seconds then stopped altogether.

'OHHHH NOOOOOOOOOOOOOOOOOOOOOOOOOOOOO!!!!' yelled Xxxmas as the sleigh dropped like a buffalo belly-flopping into a bath.

'YAAAAAAAAAAAAAAAAAAAAAAAAAA,' screamed the crook and the maggots in his beard got into the crash position. The sleigh tumbled through the air and came smashing down on to the nearest roof, sending bricks, timber and dozens of satellite dishes plummeting to the ground. This wasn't just any old roof. It was the roof of Tumchester police station.

'***Ooooooooooooooohh***,' groaned Father Xxxmas, who had found himself upside down in the chimney, with only his boots sticking out of the top. A few feet away, just the back end of the sleigh was visible, the other half was hanging through the ceiling of the police canteen.

'Er, Sarge . . .' shouted a voice from inside the station, 'you're not going to believe this . . .'

Meanwhile, Nightingale fluttered down on to the roof to check on Slug Boy. He wriggled out of the exhaust pipe and Nightingale gave his sooty nose a wipe.

'Nice job,' she said. 'As a tennis ball, you were ace!'

'Thanks,' he replied. 'All part of the *service*. Get it?'

Nightingale smiled and she would have given him a high five, except he didn't have any hands. She popped Slug Boy back into the Slugmobile and soon the Fish Fingers were reunited at the grotto. Their hour of superhero power was up and Gary, Bel, Ruby and Morris were back to normal.

Gary grinned. 'Guys, that was well cool, well sick and well epic.'

'We are the awesome foursome,' laughed Ruby.

'We do seem to be getting the hang of this superhero business don't we?' said Bel. Everybody smiled. It felt like they were.

'Come on,' said Morris. 'I'm hungry and we've got things to do.'

Morris was right. They had lots of things to do for the next day because it was going to be big. So big that their lives would never be quite the same again.

WHEN THE CHIPS ARE DOWN

The next morning, as the sun peered down at Castle Gristle like an eerie eyeball, Grubski checked his calendar. There was a big pink ring around the date. 'Time to wake the boys,' he said to himself. 'Those kids from over the foam will be on their way soon. Who'd have thought six years, four months, two weeks and five days could fly by so fast?'

There were two cages in the middle of the lab and inside lay Grubski's hired help: Bigfoot and Frogurt. These two weren't the liveliest of henchmen. In fact, they were dead. Both of them were technically deader than two dead ducks playing a game of 'Who's the Deadest Duck?' at a dead boring party. They had been ever since a nasty lawnmower accident.

But Grubski wasn't the maddest scientist in town for nothing and he'd found a way to bring them back to life whenever there was dirty work to do. Bigfoot and Frogurt were held together with bolts, superglue, Sellotape, Blu-tac, Plasticine and melted ice lolly.

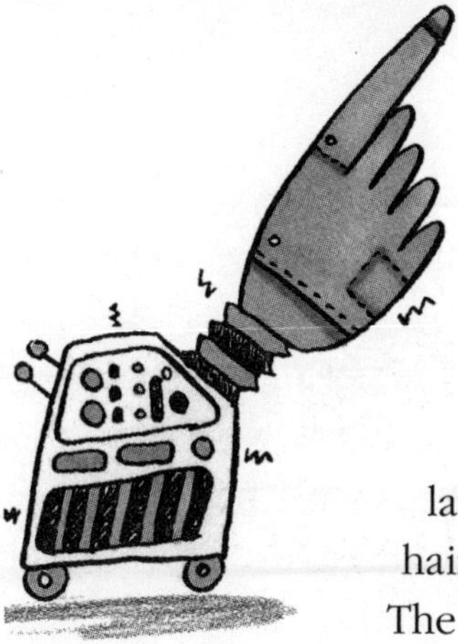

Grubski trundled a machine like a huge, silver finger over to the first cage. Bigfoot McShoe lay there, mad, bad and hairier than a barber's floor. The scientist jammed the end of the machine into a bolt sticking out of Bigfoot's neck and flicked a switch. Fireworks flew, shelves shook and flies in the fridge fainted. Slowly, the dead henchman opened his bloodshot eyes and, as his lungs filled with breath, he uttered the words . . .

'Got any chips?'

'Wait for Frogurt,' replied Grubski.

'But I need chips!' Bigfoot moaned. 'Chips, chips, chips!!'

'He won't be long,' said Grubski.

Bigfoot huffed.

Bigfoot McShoe was a supervillain with one very big foot and one very big shoe. He'd have been more scary if he'd had two big feet and two big shoes, but he didn't. His other foot was medium-sized. Bigfoot's mum wanted to name him Mediumsizedfoot McShoe, but his dad preferred the name Bigfoot and it really suited him. Bigfoot used his huge foot to kick his enemies into the middle of next week and sometimes the week after that. He booted them with the force of an express train and stamped on them with the power of a jackhammer. He also had to have his socks specially made.

Grubski now trundled the silver, finger-shaped machine over to the cage where his other dead henchman lay. Frogurt was shorter and fatter than Bigfoot and didn't have a single hair on his warty, green skin. He had a wide mouth and super-springy legs so he could leap over tall objects like trees, double-decker buses and giraffes (if he could ever find a giraffe. There weren't many in the frozen mountains of Transyldovia. Frogurt thought he saw one once but it turned out to be a very tall woman in a fur coat on a ladder. He jumped over her anyway). The only thing Frogurt loved more than leaping was landing, especially on his enemies, who got squished under his flabby, slimy belly. Frogurt also had a very unpleasant habit. He was a dribbler. Whenever he spoke, rivers of spittle trickled down his chin and, if he got excited, he'd shower everybody unlucky enough to be standing nearby.

Grubski stuck the huge finger-shaped machine into the bolt in Frogurt's neck. Nothing happened.

He turned the machine off and on again.

This time sparks danced, the lab shook and another dead henchman sat up. He burped, trumped, scratched his bottom and opened his green, flabby mouth. 'I want some ch . . . ch—'

'Don't tell me,' said Grubski. 'Chips?'

'I was going to say chickpea chow mein and cheesy chutney with chives,' said Frogurt.

'Really?' asked Grubski.

'**COURSE NOT!**' yelled Frogurt. '**Chippy wippy CHIIIIIPPPPPPPPPPPPSSSSS!**' He got so excited the spray from his mouth was like a fireman's hose.

'Ugh. Do you mind?' said Grubski. 'That has gone all over my shirt.'

'Er, sorry,' said Frogurt. 'I'll get a tissue. But then can I have some chips?'

Soon Bigfoot and Frogurt were sitting down to a huge plate of chips with extra chips and chips on the side. It being Transyldovia, the chips were made of beetroot, so they were purple, but they still tasted quite chippy.

After his seventeenth plate, Bigfoot looked up. 'Somebody change the TV channel. I'm sick of this show about beans on a roundabout.'

'That's my lunch,' said Grubski. 'You're watching the microwave. Again.'

Suddenly a burning smell filled the air and at the other end of the room, Frogurt was trying to put out flames from the TV as oats and milk trickled down the screen.

'Just trying to make some porridge to go with my chips!' said Frogurt, waving his bowl. 'But I think the microwave is broken.'

Grubski sighed. Bigfoot and Frogurt were exceptionally dumb, but they were also very useful and cheap. Quite literally cheap as chips.

'Right, pay attention,' said Grubski. 'Because here is the plan.'

'Before we start,' said Bigfoot. 'I want you to know that your plan, whatever it is, will be safe in our hands.'

'Unless, of course, our hands drop off,' said Frogurt.

This might have sounded like a dumb thing to say, but it had been a problem in the past. The henchmen didn't always make it home in one piece.

The doctor ignored Frogurt.

'Tonight,' he said, 'you will take the first step in fulfilling a 300-year-old prophecy that will change history. Tonight you will kidnap a pig.'

'Hold it right there,' said Bigfoot. 'We're not nabbing a child. Me and Frogurt are villains, always have been, always will be.'

'Will be,' said Frogurt.

'But pignapping a kid, we will not do. Kids are out of bounds.'

'Out of bounds,' echoed Frogurt.

'I didn't say pignap a kid, I said *kid*nap a *pig*,' repeated the doctor.

'Righty-ho!' said Bigfoot.

'Lefty-hee!' said Frogurt.

The doctor took a deep breath. 'But it is not just any pig you are kidnapping. This one is very special and she belongs to the Chief of Police.'

'Er, hang on,' said Bigfoot. 'Did you say the Chief of Police?'

LEAVING HOME

It was such a chilly morning in Tumchester that even the little robins could see their breath. On Fish Street most curtains were still drawn, but the Fish Fingers were wide awake and getting ready for their school ski trip to Transyldovia. The bus was leaving in less than an hour.

At number 27, Gary had crammed his rucksack full of his trendiest gear. He'd packed his skinny jeans, his orange socks and his wraparound sunglasses, but there was one thing missing – his Tumchester United hat. He was turning his bedroom upside down.

'Dad!' Gary shouted. 'I've looked everywhere!'

'Problem solved!' his dad announced, walking in with a big chef's hat, covered in grubby food stains. 'It's from when I worked at the café. It'll keep your ears warm.'

'I'm not wearing that,' said Gary. 'I'd rather stick Grandma's pants on my head.'

'This hat could save your life if you were lost on a mountain and one of your ears was getting frostbite,' said his dad.

Gary ignored him, so his dad put on a posh newsreader's voice.

'In an interview from his hospital bed Gary Gamble told reporters, "It was so cold on that mountain I thought I would lose my ears, but my dad's hat saved me. If it wasn't for his hat, I'd be saying pardon a lot and my sunglasses would keep falling off my head."'

'***DAD!*** **WILL YOU PACK IT IN!**' shouted Gary, but he couldn't help laughing. His dad was so *un*funny, he was somehow funny.

'Sorry, son,' said his dad. 'Look, it's time to go. Buy a new hat when you get there.'

He handed his son some extra pocket money.

'Thanks,' said Gary, smiling.

Just down the road at number 33, Bel's house, a classical CD tinkled softly while Bel's parents moved around their daughter like waiters. They were kind, but far too fussy, so Bel had to be very patient with them. Bel was just finishing a plate of scrambled eggs and smoked salmon.

'Another glass of orange juice, sweetheart?' asked Bel's dad.

'Or would you prefer mango?' asked her mum. 'And there's pomegranate too.'

'No thanks,' said Bel, putting her knife and fork together. 'Just a bit more packing to do!'

She raced upstairs and opened her shiny red case. It was nearly as big as a telephone box and crammed with clothes. Bel took her favourite sari from the wardrobe and held it in front of the mirror. The dress was bright green with gold embroidery and it glittered when the light caught it. She slipped it in her enormous case.

'Phew! Just fits!' she said.

A few doors down, at 36 Fish Street, Ruby was hugging her mum and dad goodbye and her gran was zipping up her suitcase.

Ruby called to her parrot, 'See you, Marvin!' and he squawked back,

'MAAAAAAARRRVIN'S STAAAAAAARVING!!!'

'Come on, my girl,' said Ruby's gran, already out of the door.

'I can't wait to get there!' said Ruby, catching up.

'Nor me,' said her gran. 'I haven't been to the jungle for ages.'

Ruby's gran got a bit confused sometimes.

'Er, we aren't going to the jungle,' said Ruby. 'I'm going skiing with the school and you are just walking me to the bus.'

'Well knock me down with a fromage frais!' said her gran. 'I didn't need to bring my hunting rifle, then.'

From under her coat she pulled out the biggest gun Ruby had ever seen. It was also the only gun Ruby had ever seen.

'Galloping gobstoppers!!!' Ruby yelled. 'Put it away!!!!'

Her gran slid the rifle back inside her coat.

'Sorry,' she said. 'I'll keep it in here with my hankies and my reading glasses.'

At 61 Fish Street, Morris was so excited that he had butterflies in his stomach. In fact he was so fluttery it felt like there were moths, ladybirds and a family of badgers in there too.

Morris's mum was in the kitchen burning toast and reading an article called 'How To Knit A Teapot' in her *Extreme Knitting* magazine. Morris waddled in and squeezed into a chair.

'Toast for breakfast,' said Morris's mum, handing him a plate of black crumbs.

'Er, thanks,' said Morris, coughing through the smoke.

'Have you put weight on?' asked his mum. 'Must be too much of my lovely cuisine. Make sure you get some exercise in Transyldovia.'

'I'll try,' said Morris, spooning up his toast. His mum was right about him gaining weight, but it was nothing to do with her food. Morris was wearing three shirts, four pairs of socks, four jumpers, three vests and five pairs of underpants (including one pair of fleece-lined long-johns).

Morris knew that Transyldovia was famous for two things: beetroot and vampires. Morris didn't believe in vampires, so he wasn't worried about them, but he did believe in beetroots and he was extremely worried about *them*. He hated beetroot. Apparently Transyldovians sometimes ate beetroot for breakfast, dinner and tea, so Morris had packed his suitcase with donuts, crisps and chocolate to make sure he didn't go hungry. It didn't leave much room for clothes, so he was wearing as many as he could.

'Take your ski goggles off at the table,' said his mum. 'It's not hygienic.'

ALL ABOARD

Gary was the first to board the bus and he quickly made his way to the back seats, where he bagged spaces for himself and the other Fish Fingers. Then Ruby and her gran arrived, skipping along the road like best friends. Ruby's gran gave her a goodbye cuddle and pressed a little present into her hand. 'Open it on the bus,' she said as Ruby bounded up the steps. Bel came next, her mum and dad carrying her case like a valuable oil painting. Mrs Pompidoor, the headteacher greeted Bel warmly.

'A *very, very* good morning to you, our guest of honour!'

Mrs Pompidoor was a large woman with round glasses and a beaky nose so she looked like a woodpigeon. Today she was wearing a yellow ski-suit, so she looked like a woodpigeon who'd been swallowed by a banana.

'Have I told you how proud we are of you, Bel?' she said.

Bel smiled. 'Yes Mrs Pompidoor. Thank you very much.'

It was only thanks to Bel that the school trip was happening at all. She'd won a competition to make a poster about the wonders of Transyldovia and the top prize was a week's holiday there for her whole class. Bel's design was a snow scene with the sun painted like a beetroot (the national symbol of Transyldovia). It was the best picture she'd ever done.

'I had an email yesterday,' said Mrs Pompidoor. 'From the *Transyldovian Times.* They want to interview you and put your photo on the front page of the newspaper. It'll be fantabulous!'

'Wow,' said Bel. She hadn't really thought about it before, but it would be really cool to be famous.

By now, most people were in their seats. A group of girls from the junior cheerleading team were among the last. They all had ponytails and matching pink jackets and they were lucky enough to go skiing every year with their families. Skyla, Poopsy, Pinkie and Lullabye air-kissed their mums and danced on to the bus.

Gary noticed there were only a few seats left now. 'Where's Morris?' he said, starting to worry.

'He might still be asleep,' panicked Ruby.

But at that moment Morris waddled round the corner. He spotted the other Fish Fingers and he was giving them a wave when . . .

'GRR GRRRRRRR!!'

Something barked behind him. Morris span round and saw the slobbering tongue and sharp fangs of a huge black dog. The beast was sprinting towards him and it seemed to think Morris was its breakfast.

'GRRR GRRR GRRR GRRR GRRRRR!!!'

It was closing in fast.

'GRRR GRRR GRRR GRR GRRRR!!!!!!'

Morris tried to run, but he was wearing so many clothes he tripped and fell, spilling everything from his case. The dog ran faster. Morris could almost feel its breath on his neck.

'**BELCHER, SIT!**' shouted a voice.

But Belcher didn't sit. Instead Belcher leapt, body stretching, teeth gnashing, tongue drooling. Morris braced himself . . .

BANG.

A noise like a crack of thunder rang out. The dog froze. The dog was scared stiff as a skateboard and it dropped, whimpering, to the ground. The crowd by the bus looked at the sky and put their brollies up, muttering, 'Sounds like a storm brewing.'

Confused, and still a bit petrified, Morris staggered to his feet. And as he did, he found himself staring into the faces of Charlie 'Snoddy' Snodgrass, schoolboy gangster, and his lanky sidekick Ferret.

'You big dork, Doris!' laughed Snoddy, flashing his chisel teeth and patting Belcher on the head. 'Soz. He slipped his leash.'

'I don't think so,' said Morris.

'Chill out, Doris, it was an accident,' said Ferret, gold chains jangling. Then he winked at Snoddy.

'That mutt is a menace,' said Morris.

Snoddy gave Morris a little push. 'Who are you calling a menace?' he snarled, but just then Mrs Pompidoor interrupted.

'Hello, Charles. Hello, Peter. Hurry up, Morris. You three are the last. Time to be off.'

Morris gathered up his things. *Snoddy and Ferret did that on purpose*, he thought. *Lucky that crack of thunder happened when it did. Although it doesn't really look like rain . . .*

Five minutes later all the mums, dads, grans and grandads cheered, 'Bye!!!' as the coach set off. Some waved hankies, others wiped tears from their eyes. Ruby's gran patted the hunting rifle, now back in her coat.

I knew it would come in handy, she thought and skipped off home.

A RIGHT PIG'S HERE

'The Chief Constable's pig lives in a top-security barn at police HQ,' Grubski announced. 'As you know, police HQ is surrounded by a moat and razor wire.'

Bigfoot chortled and Frogurt guffawed.

'Do you mind?' said Dr Grubski to Frogurt. 'You've done it again. Spittle all over the floor.'

'Sorry,' said Frogurt. 'I'll get a cloth.'

Pot-bellied pigs were a very popular pet in Transyldovia, but they were also particularly useful to the police. Trandsyldovian pigs have a highly developed sense of smell. They can trace the whiff of a stolen object buried deep underground or follow the trail left by a criminal weeks after the crook has gone. The Transyldovian police force had a special team of sniffer pigs and among them was a real superstar. She'd caught dozens of crooks and won hundreds of medals. Her name was Mee.

'I'll break it down for you again,' said Grubski.

'Step 1: Fly in the invisible airship to police headquarters.'

'Right,' said Bigfoot.

'Step 2: Lower yourselves into the barn through a hole in the roof,' said Grubski.

'Got it,' said Frogurt.

'Step 3: Steal Mee.'

'Steal you, doctor?' said Bigfoot. 'We couldn't do that. We like you!'

'And we couldn't sell you even if we stole you,' said Frogurt. 'Not much call for mad doctors on e-Bay.'

'Not me. *Mee!*' said Grubski.

'Not you, you? That doesn't make sense,' said Bigfoot.

'Mee is a pig,' said Grubski.

'You is a pig?' said Frogurt. 'I thought you was a doctor!'

'I *IS* A DOCTOR!! *AM* A DOCTOR!!!' said Grubski. '**YOU NEED TO STEAL THE PIG, MEE!**'

'No need to shout,' said Bigfoot.

'He's a long way from home,' said Frogurt.

'Who is?' said Grubski.

'This pygmy,' said Frogurt. 'I thought those little fellas lived in the jungle.'

'**NOT A PYGMY!!!! THE PIG, MEE. MEE IS A PIG!!!!**'

'But I thought you was . . .'

This conversation went on for most of the day.

By nightfall it was at last time to put the plan into action. Under the moon's ghoulish glow, Bigfoot, Frogurt and Grubski stood at the bottom of the steps leading to the invisible airship. This huge, egg-shaped balloon with its sleek cockpit was one of Grubski's greatest inventions. The airship had the power to blend in with the sky, so it was impossible to see from the ground. At this moment it was black and starry but in the day it could be anything from cloudy to bright blue. Fiendishly clever, just like Grubski himself.

'The pigs all sleep in the barn together,' explained the doctor. 'But Mee sleeps on a pink cushion and she has three little spots under her belly.'

Bigfoot and Frogurt nodded.

'One last thing,' said Grubski. 'Keep out of the mini-bar. You know what happened last time.'

The henchmen looked at each other and blushed.

As they entered the cockpit, Bigfoot elbowed Frogurt out of the way and jumped behind the steering wheel. 'I am the hairiest, so I'll be driving,' he said.

'Well that makes sense,' nodded Frogurt.

This left Frogurt in charge of the radio, the mints and the air freshener, so he quickly got bored. 'I hate long journeys,' he said. 'Are we there yet?' but since they hadn't even left the ground, they weren't there yet.

Grubski untied the anchor ropes and the airship rose over the castle walls and drifted into the night.

The doctor phoned his evil twin.

'They've just gone,' he said.

'Good,' said the deep, dark voice on the other end. 'Call me as soon as they are back.'

'They won't fail us,' said Grubski.

'They'd better not,' replied the voice.

Bigfoot and Frogurt soon turned their attention to the mini-bar. The little fridge was full of extremely fizzy Transyldovian beetroot squash.

'A shame we can't have any,' said Frogurt.

'That would be stealing,' said Bigfoot. 'And, as the captain of the ship, I can't allow it.'

'None for us then,' sighed Frogurt.

'Of course, if I gave you a bottle that wouldn't be stealing. *That* would be generous,' said Bigfoot. 'Which I can allow.'

'And if I gave you a bottle *that* would be generous too. The Doc wouldn't mind if we did something kind like that. Hee hee hee,' said Frogurt.

'Just one bottle each, though,' warned Bigfoot.

'Yes, yes. Just one, hee hee hee,' said Frogurt, spittle splatting on the windscreen.

The airship flew high above Transyldovia's most famous mountain, the Flugelhorn, and the two henchmen looked down, their noses pressed against the window. The south side of the Flugelhorn was where the sun shone, skiers skied and the smell of warm beetroot milkshake filled the air. The north side was full of dark caves, wolves and prickle trees. They were separated by the Great Flugel Falls in the east and a deep ravine called Dead Man's Throat in the west. Dead Man's Throat was the most dangerous place in Transyldovia and it had gobbled up countless climbers in its time.

A little while later, the airship floated silently above the police pig barn and the villains got out their binoculars. As they peered down at the guards in the towers, the razor wire and the moat they started to giggle.

'It's supposed to be top security,' said Bigfoot. 'But we're sneaking in as easy as a piece of easy-peasy pie.'

'Even easier than that!' said Frogurt. 'Two pieces of easy-peasy pie!'

'Even easier than that!' said Bigfoot. 'Three pieces of easy-peasy pie!'

'Easier than that!' said Frogurt. 'Four pieces of easy-peasy pie!'

Down below, Chief Constable Alexis Viddle was inspecting the guards. She was a short woman with short hair and a short temper and she always wore mirror sunglasses, so it was impossible to know whether she was happy or sad. Her hands were as big as shovels and her body looked like it was made of bricks and when she was angry she whispered. This was even scarier than when she shouted.

Viddle strode along the line of nervous guards. 'There isn't a criminal mastermind whose mind is a master of my mind and if you don't mind, there never will be. Is that clear?'

The guards nodded. It wasn't very clear, but they were too petrified to admit it.

Viddle stopped suddenly. 'Brewski, is that . . . beetroot custard on your tie?' she whispered.

Brewski's bottom lip trembled. 'Er, it c-could b-be Chief. I had beetroot trifle for pudding.'

Police regulations, section 4, subsection 2: No guard shall report for duty wearing beetroot custard or other runny foodstuffs. This includes beetroot gravy, beetroot ketchup and beetroot barbecue sauce.

'You can look yourself in your cell on your day off,' Viddle whispered.

'Y-y-yes Chief, sorry Chief,' said Brewski.

Chief Viddle marched off to the pig barn. It was time to say good night to her beloved Mee. The little pig had been a birthday present from her dad and the gift had changed her life. It was thanks to Mee's brilliant snout that Viddle had caught countless crooks and risen from lowly police officer to Chief Constable.

'Nighty night, my princess,' she said before tucking her in. Mee snuggled down happily on her pink cushion and Viddle walked back to her office.

In the invisible airship overhead, Bigfoot and Frogurt were deep in conversation.

'Five thousand, seven hundred and sixty one pieces of easy-peasy pie!' said Bigfoot.

'Even easier than that!' said Frogurt. 'Five thousand, seven hundred and sixty two pieces of easy-peasy pie!'

'Even easier than that!' said Bigfoot. 'Five thousand, seven hundred and sixty . . .'

They were interrupted by the shrill trrrrrriiiiing of Bigfoot's phone.

It was Grubski. 'Have you got the pig yet?' he said.

'Who, me?' answered Bigfoot.

'Yes, Mee,' said Grubski.

'Yes, you?' asked Bigfoot.

'Don't start that again you idiot!' shouted Grubski. 'Is the pig with you?'

'We've only just arrived,' said Bigfoot. 'We're hovering over police HQ.'

'Fine,' said Grubski. 'Put the ship on autopilot and don't waste any more time.'

Bigfoot and Frogurt climbed down on to the lowest deck of the airship. They opened an exit hatch to the outside and dropped a long ladder down to the roof of the pig barn. Slowly, silently, they clambered down, clutching their flashlights, a hacksaw and a net.

Once they'd cut a hole in the barn roof they dropped through on to the muddy floor and looked around. It was a bit whiffy, but the pigs were all asleep, snoring peacefully. They spotted Mee, snoozing on her pink cushion.

The henchmen looked at each other and grinned. So far, so good. But as they tiptoed over, the sweet smell of success gave way to a different kind of whiff. If only they'd stopped drinking at one bottle of fizzy beetroot squash. Then it might have been okay. But since they glugged the entire contents of the mini-bar, eruptions on a volcanic scale were just a matter of time.

STINK BOMBS

It started slowly.

Squrp

'Did you step on a squeaky floorboard?' asked Bigfoot.

'No, sorry,' said Frogurt, blushing. 'That was me. I, er, trumped.'

'Well don't do it again, or you'll wake the pigs,' said Bigfoot.

Quarrrraaaarrrrkk

'Is there a duck in here?' asked Frogurt. 'I think I just heard a duck.'

'I dropped one,' said Bigfoot.

'You dropped a duck?' asked Frogurt.

'No, I trumped like you,' said Bigfoot. 'You've set me off. But it won't happen again. Let's get on with it.'

Squiiirrrrrrrrrrrrrppp!

'Cough! . . . ahem, ahem.' Frogurt tried coughing to cover it up, but even Bigfoot wasn't dumb enough to fall for that.

'That's horrible,' said Bigfoot. 'You should be ashamed of yourself. It's making my eyes water!'

'Sorry,' said Frogurt, ashamed.

ffffaarrrrrrrrrrrrrrrrrrpppp!!

(That was Bigfoot.)

'Uuuggghhh!' said Frogurt. 'That's the worst yet. The paint's peeling off the walls.'

Not surprisingly, before Bigfoot and Frogurt got within a few steps of Mee, the poor pig was wide awake and she didn't like what she could smell. Neither did the other pigs and soon they were all grunting, squealing and whizzing around like pink dodgems at a fairground.

'Stop little – ffffaarrrrrrrrrrrrrrrrrrpppp!! – piggy!' Bigfoot called softly. He couldn't shout because the guards outside might hear.

Frogurt hissed, 'Come b— ffffffweeeeeeeeeeeeepp!! —ack, oh no!'

The villains soon lost track of which pig was Mee. At the speed the animals were running they all looked the same. They were also getting dirtier and dirtier.

'This is – **twaaaaaaaarrrrrrrrrrpp!!** – her isn't it?' said Bigfoot, chasing after one little piggy, but then planting his big foot in something horrible and slipping over.

'No, I think that's – **prrrrrrrrrrrraaaappp!!** – her over there,' said Frogurt pointing at another piggy. 'Oh, I don't – **prrrrrruuuuuuup** – know.'

Suddenly the two supervillains froze. There were voices outside. Two guards had heard the commotion and were coming in.

'Sounds like there's a duck in there,' said one of the guards. He pulled open the door but then immediately slammed it shut.

'**Zowweeee**. Something hasn't agreed with them. Let's leave it until the whiff's died down.'

Bigfoot and Frogurt breathed again.

'Okay, we've got – **purrrrrrrpp!!** – a few minutes before those guards come back,' said Bigfoot. 'If we nab the wrong pig we'll be in big trouble. So we'll just have to – **fuuurrrpp!!** – kidnap them all.'

'You've got to be – **trrrraaaarrpp!!** – joking,' said Frogurt. 'There must be over twenty pigs in here!' He started counting on his fingers. 'There's three there . . . plus two . . . one there . . . borrow from the tens . . . Minus that . . . carry the one . . .' he muttered, giving up. 'Whatever it is, it's definitely more than I've got fingers.'

'No choice but to take them,' said Bigfoot. 'And – **peeeeepppaaah!!** – the sooner we start, the sooner we'll begin.'

Frogurt nodded. Bigfoot was so wise sometimes.

Squeep.

BUSY ON THE BUS

On the Fish Street School bus, the children had been having a lovely time. The driver was a tall Jamaican man called Wilbert who sang reggae songs into the on-board microphone and even Mrs Pompidoor joined in.

There was one sour note though and it came from somewhere very unexpected, best friends Bel and Ruby.

Soon after they'd left, Ruby unwrapped the present her gran had given her. It was a brilliant new camera.

'Jumping jellybeans,' beamed Ruby. 'It's smashing!!' Ruby couldn't stop taking photos of the scenery outside. 'Look at the view,' she kept saying and it started to annoy Bel, who had her newspaper interview on her mind. She was thrilled to be doing it, but nervous too.

Bel asked if she could borrow the camera.

'Sure,' answered Ruby.

Bel got a pair of sunglasses from her bag and popped them on. Then she held the camera at arm's length and took a selfie. She changed her expression from a big smile with teeth to a thin smile without teeth and took another. Then she swapped the sunglasses for a glittery hairband and took yet another. Bel seemed to have an endless supply of accessories and an endless supply of smiles.

Eventually, Ruby said, 'Can I have my camera back now?'

'Just one more,' said Bel. 'I'm trying to find my best look for the newspaper.' She pressed the button again, and the battery died.

'Well thanks very much,' said Ruby grabbing back her camera.

'No need to snatch,' said Bel.

'No need to take so many selfies,' said Ruby.

The girls sat in silence for a while. It was broken by the noise of what sounded like someone sawing logs with a trombone. Morris was snoring; his mouth was open and his tongue was hanging out. Bel and Ruby looked at each other and giggled. Then they hugged. 'Sorry!' they said together and instantly, they were friends again.

Once the bus had taken the ferry across the foamy sea, Wilbert put his foot down and it wasn't long before the road signs went from French to German, Romanian, Albanian and at last to Transyldovian. Soon the sun was rising and the children all gave a big cheer when they went over the last border. They whooped even louder when they drove past a billboard with Bel's *Transport Me to Transyldovia* poster on. Mrs Pompidoor celebrated by handing round cups of beetroot milkshake. ('**UGGGHH!**' said Morris. 'And so it begins, death by beetroot.')

They hit the twisty, turny mountain road that took them up, up, up towards the town of Flugelville. Snow was everywhere, lying thick and soft. From the windows of the coach the Fish Fingers gazed out on a magical world. The fields seemed like they were made of marshmallow and the trees looked like they'd been dipped in ice cream. Up, up, up the curvy mountain road. So high now even the grown-ups got a little scared. They stared down at the valley hundreds of feet below and it gave everybody a shiver.

'We'll be arriving in Flugelville in a few minutes,' announced Mrs Pompidoor. 'So take the chance to enjoy the scenery. In the distance you can see the ruins of Castle Gristle where the legendary vampire Vladi the Baddie lived. No such thing as vampires,

of course, but a fantabulous story!'

She pointed out lots of little wooden huts that dotted the landscape. 'They are called *tinklehouzen* and that's where you can er, take a tinkle!' she said. 'And in the woods you may spot rabbits, woodpeckers and er . . .'

The headteacher stopped. Because she was sure she'd just seen a flying pig.

No, that would be impossible, she said to herself.

Mrs Pompidoor carried on. 'Er, you can see rabbits, woodpeckers and ***LOOK OUT IT'S A FLYING PIIIIG!***'

THUDDDD OINK. The creature hit the windscreen.

THUDDDD OINK. Wilbert swerved and the children shrieked as another pig crash-landed on the roof. The driver slammed on the brakes, but the bus was now skidding dangerously. Everyone screamed. The bus span towards the edge of the mountain road. Wilbert wrestled with the steering wheel. The coach lurched on to two wheels, smashed into a boulder and flipped on to its roof. As it skidded across the icy road

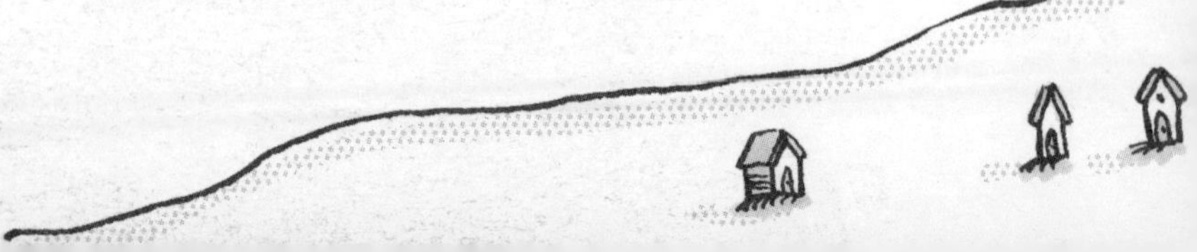

it made a noise like cats' claws scraping down a window. Far, far below only rocks, river and prickle trees. The children screamed again, waiting for the worst. Then, suddenly, the bus stopped. Everyone breathed deeply. Bumped and bruised, nothing more serious. But as they opened their eyes, they could see they weren't completely safe yet. The back of the bus was on the road, but the front was hanging over the side of the mountain.

The children all dangled upside down in their seats, blood rushing to their heads.

'Stay calm and stay where you are,' Wilbert called but there wasn't much choice. Anyone who undid their seatbelt would fall and bang their heads on the roof that was now the floor. So everybody was stuck.

Except the superheroes. Luckily, they were sitting at the back of the bus, so nobody else saw what happened next. Morris shrank to slug size and dropped down silently, Gary slipped out of his seatbelt like an acrobat, Bel felt herself fluttering into the air and Ruby bounced softly from her seat. Transformations complete, they dashed through the emergency exit.

Once outside, the Fish Fingers stood and blinked. They'd never seen anything like it. The clouds were raining pigs. Little pot-bellied ones, black and pink, falling like raindrops. Transyldovian pigs are particularly bouncy and they were landing in soft snow so they weren't hurt, but they weren't enjoying it either. OIIIIINK was the sound as they fell from the sky. **THUDDD** as they hit the ground. OINK as they got up and ran off. Nightingale found the two that had crashed into the bus. They were trotting up the road and looked a bit

grumpy, but they would be okay.

'Come on,' said The Chimp, 'We've got to –'

OIIIIINK. **THUD** OINK.

He was hit on the head by a flying pig and fell face down in the snow, too dazed to move.

KangaRuby quickly put her hand in her pocket and pulled out . . . a teapot. It wasn't much help, especially as there wasn't any tea in it. But there was something buzzing in the spout. A wasp. Wasps don't like the cold and this one had been very happy in KangaRuby's warm pocket. It was now seriously grouchy and it shot out of the spout ready to sting the first thing it could see – KangaRuby's nose.

'Jeepers! Ow ow ow ow!!!' she cried and sat down to rub her nose with snow.

Nightingale rocketed into the air, with Slug Boy in the Slugmobile. Two Fish Fingers were down, but there were still two left. That was until Nightingale crashed headfirst into the bottom of the invisible airship. Luckily she missed the blades of the propeller, but it was still a big bump. She fluttered in the air for a second, trying to work out what she'd flown in to. Looking up she saw two faces that seemed to be floating in the clouds. Nightingale had never seen anything so ugly – one had beady eyes with a bristly beard, the other had green skin and a gruesome, dribbly mouth.

'AAAAGGGHHHH!! GHOSTS!!!' she screamed.

It was too much for Nightingale, who flapped down into the snow and sat there fanning herself.

Sitting in the Slugmobile, which was still strapped to Nightingale's arm, Slug Boy felt a bit stuck on his own. Nonetheless, he flipped open the lid and slithered out. He'd rescued them all before, and he could do it again. 'Slug Boy to the rescue!' he shouted. Then the cold hit him. Within seconds he was stiffer than a stick of seaside rock. Too frozen even to wriggle.

By the time the police and the mountain rescue team arrived, the Fish Fingers were back to normal. Gary, Morris, Ruby and Bel were all found sitting outside the bus, shivering in the snow. They got told off by the police and Mrs Pompidoor for not listening to Wilbert and staying safe inside. A special crane brought the coach back on to the road before everybody was taken into Flugelville by taxi. Wilbert went to hospital with a broken wrist.

'I think we'll spend the rest of the day at the hotel,' said Mrs Pompidoor to the class. 'We've had more than enough excitement for one morning.'

On the way back, none of the Fish Fingers said

very much. They had thought they were getting good at being superheroes, but today they felt like beginners all over again.

When the police heard about the flying pigs they were astonished. And when they discovered it was *their* sniffer pigs they were flabbergasted. They'd been searching for the pigs for the last two hours and the last thing they expected was to find them dropping out of the sky. Chief Viddle began frantically checking each one.

'Where's Mee? Where's Mee?' she whispered as the police pigs were rounded up but it didn't take the Chief long to realise that Mee was missing. Viddle was so angry she punched herself on the nose. It must have really hurt, but nobody could tell because she was wearing her mirror sunglasses. The Chief called her officers together. 'Right,' she whispered.

A TRANSYLDOVIAN'S HOME IS HIS CASTLE

Bigfoot and Frogurt sat in the cockpit of the airship, floating back to Castle Gristle and tucking into some cold chips they always kept in their pockets. Their violent trumps had subsided into just occasional toots, Mee was asleep in a basket and soon it would be mission accomplished.

Still, it had been a long night. Stealing all the police pigs had seemed like a good idea at the time, but once on board the henchmen soon realised they couldn't take every single one back home.

'Grubski will go nutski if these little piggies start running around his lab,' Frogurt had said. 'Then he'll say to us "No chips all weekend" or maybe "No chips for a month of Sundays" or "No chips for a week of Wednesdays". I don't like it Bigfoot, I don't like it at all.'

'Okay,' said his partner. 'Here's what we'll do. Give them a bath, find the one with the spots, then throw the others out of the window. Isn't there a saying about pigs might fly? So they might.'

So that was what Bigfoot and Frogurt did. They hadn't expected the Fish Street School bus to come up the road at just the wrong moment, but it didn't do any harm. In fact, the henchmen had found it all very entertaining.

'All's well that begins well,' said Bigfoot wisely.

'Yes and curiosity kissed the cat,' said Frogurt.

'A bird in the hand is worth two in the bush,' said Bigfoot. 'But it might poop on your fingers.'

'And that's how you get bird flu,' said Frogurt.

It was lucky the airship touched down just then or they would have been wittering on all week.

Dr Grubski was outside waiting. He guessed something had gone wrong because they were five hours late. But when he saw they'd arrived with the right pig and without crashing the airship he was pleased. He cooked them an enormous plate of chips to celebrate.

Grubski put a collar round Mee and walked her to the door. He said to his henchmen, 'Right, follow me.'

They looked at him blankly.

'Er, you or the pig?' asked Bigfoot.

'**JUST FOLLOW ME AND MEE**,' said Grubski. '**WE ARE BOTH GOING IN THE SAME DIRECTION!**'

'Keep your hair on,' said Bigfoot. 'Me and him can just follow Mee and you. That solves the problem.'

Grubski led them all to the lift and pressed a

button to take them down.

The doctor and his twin had spent years tunnelling underneath the castle and there were floors and secret tunnels in all directions. Grubski took them past suits of armour and paintings of old men with long noses. Bats screeched in the shadows and spiders crept in the corners. As they went further into the bowels of the building, the walls were just rock and the light just a few flickering candles.

'Pick your feet up,' Grubski said to Bigfoot, who was clomping along.

'I'm being as quick as I can,' Bigfoot answered.

'JUST PICK YOUR FEET UP!' shouted the doctor.

'I can't help it,' said Bigfoot. 'I'm a big guy in big shoes. Well, one big shoe.'

The doctor sighed. 'Pick your feet up, because they've dropped off your legs!'

Bigfoot looked round and saw his feet yards back down the tunnel. 'Oh yeah,' he said and clomped off to pick them up.

'Tie them on with string for now,' said Grubski. 'I'll fix them later.'

Soon they came to a rusty door in the shape of a skull and Grubski was about to open it when his mobile phone rang.

'Where are you my brother?' asked his evil twin.

'We're outside the Great Hall,' said Grubski. 'I've come for the sock.'

'Good,' said the voice. 'And it's probably time you told those numbskulls a bit more about the prophecy. Not that they'll understand it, of course. But if you keep henchmen in the dark too long they tend to fall over and break things.'

The doctor turned the handle on the iron door and led Bigfoot, Frogurt and Mee inside the Great Hall. It was the kind of room where you'd expect to see the Queen of England dancing with the King of Spain as the Emperor of Japan played piano. There were crystal chandeliers,

gold statues and precious paintings. But Bigfoot and Frogurt didn't really notice the decor. They were too busy staring at the massive dinosaur skeletons.

'I-is th-that th-thing real?' asked Bigfoot, gazing at a particularly nasty-looking Tyrannosaurus rex.

'Of course,' answered Grubski. 'He's got sixty teeth, each one sharp enough to saw meat and strong enough to crack bone.'

'I think I'll p-p-pop back to the lab now,' said Frogurt. 'I suffer from giant-scary-dinosaur-bone-aphobia. Everyone in my family has got it.'

'Stay where you are,' said Grubski. 'He is perfectly harmless and even deader than you are. I collect dead things. It is why I have a soft spot for you two.'

Bigfoot and Frogurt gave the T-rex a careful tap and he did sound very dead. They relaxed a little and took in the other dinosaur in the room. There was a brilliant brontosaurus, a stunning stegosaurus, a towering triceratops and a pterrific pterodactyl.

'Enough sight-seeing,' said Grubski. 'We need to get down to business.' He took Vladi the Baddie's diary from his pocket and held it up. 'This was written by the most brilliant leader our country has ever known, a president who struck fear into the hearts of millions, a supervillain called **VLADI THE BADDIE**.'

'We know all about him,' said Bigfoot.

'We did him at school,' said Frogurt.

'Good,' said Grubski. 'Then you'll know he was also secretly a va—'

'Van driver, yes,' said Frogurt.

'No,' said Grubski. 'A va—'

'Vacuum cleaner repairman, we know, very scary,' said Bigfoot.

'**A VAMPIRE you dodos!**' yelled Grubski.

'Oh *that* Vladi the Baddie,' said Bigfoot.

'We didn't know you meant *him*,' said Frogurt.

Grubski carried on. 'It is Vladi's prophecy, written in these pages, that we are going to fulfil. When we do, we'll transform Transyldovia into a nation of zombies and rule the country forever.'

Bigfoot grinned and Frogurt laughed, sending a spray of spittle all over the brontosaurus skeleton.

Grubski took a deep breath. 'You shall now hear the chilling prophecy in its entirety.' He assumed a solemn expression and began to read . . .

This Book Belongs to . . . Vladi T. Baddie.
Happy birthday, love Nan.

'Wow,' breathed Bigfoot.

'Best prophecy I've ever heard,' spat Frogurt.

'Er, sorry, wrong page,' said Grubski, flicking through the book. 'Here we are, the prophecy . . .

My Prophecy :)

Ye Will Have EVERLASTING POWER if Ye FOLLOW These Steps

300 years from my jubilee
Sniff out a vampire under a treee
Get a class of kids from over the foam
And feed them soup with a dinosaur bone

Give the kids a nasty wedgie
Then sprinkle their blood on a famous veggie
Smother it in the vampire's sneeze
And grate it up to look like cheese

Mix it into the city's drinking,
And the folks won't know what they're thinking
Their brains will be washed, their eyes will be DEAD,
But they'll think you're the best thing since sliced . . .
beetroot.

'I like it,' said Bigfoot. 'But I think I preferred the first one about his Nan.'

'Is it something to do with cheese on toast?' asked Frogurt.

'Don't worry yourselves,' said Grubski. 'In short we just need to raise a vampire, kidnap some kids, brainwash an entire nation and then we'll be rich. Very, very rich.'

'Hang on, there aren't any real vampires left are

SHOPPING:

* kids
* their blood
* dinosaur bones
* most famous vegetable in the world
* vampire sneeze

there?' asked Bigfoot. 'Because if there are, I am allergic to them.'

'Oh, so am I!' said Frogurt. 'Actually it's another phobia. Even worse than my giant-scary-dinosaur-bone-aphobia.'

'Baddies don't need to be afraid of other baddies,' said Grubski. 'Only goodies need to be afraid of baddies.'

Grubski and his twin had been thinking long and hard about the prophecy and now it was starting to come together at last. *Sniff out a vampire under a treee* was the reason they had stolen Mee.

'Starting tomorrow, you two and the pig will go out sniffing under all the trees on the Flugelhorn to find a vampire,' said Grubski. 'Mee will need a scent to follow and I luckily I have the perfect thing for her to smell.'

He opened a safe that was hidden behind a painting and took out a pongy, black sock. 'I found this slipped between the pages of the diary. Vladi must have used it as a bookmark.'

'I do that with my socks,' said Frogurt. 'If I can't find a chip to use.'

THINGS GO DOWNHILL FAST

After a good night's sleep, the children from Fish Street School were ready for an exciting day on the slopes. It was time to put the flying-pig-upside-down-bus incident behind them and have some fun.

Breakfast in the dining room was a lot tastier than Morris had feared. Everything involved beetroot of course – boiled beetroot, mashed beetroot, grilled beetroot – but Morris found something called *pain au chocobeetroot* and he thought it was delicious. He was queuing for his fourteenth, when the hotel manager, Mr Kreep, stopped him. 'That's more than enough boy!' he hissed, flicking his tongue out like a lizard.

Morris sat down grumpily and whispered to the others, 'I don't like that manager guy.'

'I know what you mean,' said Ruby. 'Kreep by name, creep by nature.'

At that moment Mrs Pompidoor stood up to talk to everybody. She'd swapped yesterday's yellow ski suit for an orange one so now she looked like a woodpigeon that had been swallowed by a tangerine instead of a banana.

'Good morning, everybody.'

'GOOD-MOOOOR-NING-MI-SISS-POM-PI-DOORR'

they answered like it was an assembly even though it wasn't.

'As it's your first morning,' she said, 'I want you all to take things gently. Most of you have never been on skis before, but that's nothing to worry about. Especially as we have a wonderful ski instructor! Boys and girls, give a big clap for Miss Krystal.'

The door to the dining room opened and in walked the most beautiful woman the children had ever seen. Her hair was golden, her eyes sky blue and her fluttering eyelashes were as pretty as butterflies. Bel noticed her fingernails were painted the same pink shade as hers.

'Ooh, she's so cool,' Bel whispered to Ruby.

'Listen up guys,' said Miss Krystal in a sweet American-sounding voice. 'I don't know about you, but I can't wait to get skiing. See y'all on the mountain in fifteen!'

She waved like a beauty queen as she left the room, and flashed them a sparkling smile.

The children cheered. They loved it when teachers didn't talk too much and Miss Krystal seemed to understand that. Soon they were all dressed in their ski gear and standing on the beginner's slope of the Flugelhorn. It was the perfect place to start and it even had a miniature cable car to carry them from the bottom to the top.

Gary was wearing a new dragon hat he'd bought in the hotel lobby, Bel was in powder pink and Ruby's ski suit was one of her gran's that had been repaired so many times it looked like a patchwork quilt. Morris was wearing every single item of clothing he had, including two pairs of gloves.

'Best to be on the safe side,' he said to Gary. 'Looks a bit nippy.'

Miss Krystal explained how to point their skis in a V-shape to slow down.

'Follow me,' said Miss Krystal. 'And you'll be just dandy.'

It was a wonderful morning. Zipping, zooming and falling over. They crashed and bumped, slipped and skidded into each other and rolled around in the snow, giggling until their sides hurt. Of course some were better skiers than others. Snoddy and Ferret were brilliant because they spent so much time at home skateboarding. They had natural balance and soon they were allowed to swap their skis for snowboards. Gary was just as good as them, but he wasn't such a show off. He loved weaving in and out of the trees and practising his turns. Ruby wanted to try every activity possible, one minute she was ski jumping, the next she was snowboarding, the next she was taking action photos of the others in mid-air. Bel was by far the fastest because she was utterly fearless and she loved going at top speed. The only skiers who could keep up with her were the junior cheerleaders Skyla, Poopsy, Pinkie and Lullabye. They all had matching ski suits and Bel quite enjoyed joining in with their formations. To nobody's surprise, skiing didn't come easily to Morris. Snoddy and Ferret started a competition to see who could push him over the most, but it quickly got boring because Morris was falling over so much on his own. He found dozens of new ways to come down the mountain without skis – on his back, on his bottom, head first, feet first, elbows first, pulling Mrs Pompidoor, clinging to Miss Krystal and once with his ski boot jammed in a hot dog stand, dragging a cook and seven hungry Transyldovian customers behind him.

In the afternoon they were allowed to move on to the adult slopes as Miss Krystal said they'd all made good progress (and even Morris wasn't falling over quite so much). This meant a trip further up the mountain in a huge cable car, to where the crowds were bigger, the air was thinner and the slopes were faster. Miss Krystal told them to stick to the runs marked with blue flags as they were for beginners and to keep away from the tricky red slopes. 'And never go anywhere near the black ones, guys. Those are just for experts.'

Gary, Bel and Ruby found the top of the mountain much more exciting because they could ski faster and for longer. Morris just found he could fall over faster and slide on his bottom for longer.

After a while, Mrs Pompidoor waved Bel over. 'Time for your interview with the chappy from the newspaper!' she said. The headteacher then led Bel to a little café where a reporter in a bright red shirt and silky scarf was waiting. He had a trendy moustache too that he kept twiddling.

'Hi, I'm Petrov,' he said. 'And you must be Bel. Wow, you're going to sell a ton of newspapers!'

'I am?' she asked.

'Sure,' said Petrov. 'Cute pictures sell papers. Cute dogs, cute cats, cute little old ladies and best of all, cute kids.'

Bel started to dream of being famous and the more she dreamed, the more she loved the idea.

'Sit down over by the window,' said Petrov. Mrs Pompidoor went to get a cup of tea while Petrov took lots of photographs and asked dozens of questions.

'It's a miracle you survived that bus crash,' he said. 'You're a heroine!'

'It was a lucky escape,' said Bel. 'But I didn't do anything. Our driver, Wilbert was the hero because he stopped the bus going over a cliff.'

'But he don't look like a celebrity!' laughed Petrov. 'And he didn't draw that *Transport Me To Transyldovia* poster! By the way, got any hobbies?'

'I sing in the school choir,' said Bel.

'Did you sing on the bus?' asked Petrov.

Bel couldn't remember.

'Doesn't matter,' he said and gave her a wink. 'Don't let the truth get in the way of a good story.'

Bel giggled.

Not far from the café, Morris decided to try one of the little tinklehouzen huts because he needed a *tinkle*. He pulled open the door and looked around. It was like a hotel room, with carpet on the floor, flowers in a vase, a full-length mirror and a picture of the Transyldovian president, Mr Jetski.

'It's posher than our house,' thought Morris, locking the door. But before he could take another step he felt the whole hut shudder. He tried to get out, but the door was jammed shut. The shaking got worse and the flowers tumbled out of the vase, Morris slipped and found himself sprawled on the floor like an upside-down tortoise.

'**HELLLLLP!**' he yelled, frantically trying to stand up but it was no good. Each time he tried, the tinklehouzen shook again.

SLIP SLIDING AWAY

Morris's cries for help were met with a sudden burst of laughter from outside.

Snoddy and Ferret had spotted Morris going into the tinklehouzen and seized the chance to scare him. They'd jammed the door with a stick and started shaking the little hut from side to side.

'**AVALANCHE!**' sniggered Snoddy.

'**EARTHQUAKE!!**' giggled Ferret.

Morris stumbled to his feet, but the tinklehouzen was still rocking. '***I KNOW WHO'S OUT THERE***,' he shouted. The President's picture fell off the wall, smashing on the floor and the sound of shattering glass acted like an alarm bell to the boys outside. They knew they'd gone too far.

'Time to leg it,' sniggered Ferret.

'And fast,' agreed Snoddy and they shot off down the mountain in a cloud of snow.

But the bullies had done more damage than they realised. A lot more. They'd cracked the cement that held the tinklehouzen on to the mountain and, as

Morris tried to open the door with a last big heave-ho, the whole thing toppled over.

And then it started to move.

Suddenly the little hut was on its side, sliding down the mountain, gathering speed, and Morris was trapped inside.

'**HELP!**' he screamed, but he was hurtling down the slope faster than a hungry shark chasing a giant tuna-mayo sandwich.

Morris's body started to wobble and shrink. There was no doubt about it, this was an emergency! Within seconds Morris was the size of a gherkin and slithering up the wall of the hut.

'***HEEEEEEEEEEEEEELLLLLLLLLPPPPPPPPPPPP!!!***' he screamed again.

The runaway hut went straight through a café terrace, scattering chairs and tables, before ploughing through a herd of reindeer and causing a stampede. Then it sliced the door off another tinklehouzen, much to the annoyance of the man inside who was reading a newspaper with his trousers round his ankles. As the door fell off he yelled, 'Hooligans! Vandals!' but there was no stopping the hut.

Inside, Slug Boy was panicking and with good reason. There was a tiny hole in the door and he peered out. Flashing past were trees, rocks, snow, skiers, and – most worryingly – black flags. Black flags only meant one thing. He was out of control on one of the Flugelhorn's deadliest slopes. 'Only for expert skiers,' Miss Krystal had said. Definitely not the place for a runaway tinklehouzen!

'**SLUG BOY! ARE YOU IN THERE?**' came a voice from outside the door. Slug Boy could barely hear over the whooshing air, but he knew it was Nightingale.

From the window of the café Bel had seen the tinklehouzen fall and spotted Ferret and Snoddy dashing away. She knew they must have been up to no good so, while Petrov and Mrs Pompidoor chatted, Bel had slipped outside and started skiing after the hut. It wasn't long before her superpowers kicked in and she was flying alongside.

'**I'M IN HERE!**' shouted Slug Boy. '**WHAT'S THE PLAN?**'

'Er, haven't got one,' said Nightingale.

'Er, can you think of one?!' yelled Slug Boy. 'Because if you don't, ***I'M GOING TO BE SMASHED TO SMITHEREENS!!***'

Nightingale took a deep breath. Then she spotted two big metal nails jutting out of the back of the tinklehouzen. Big enough to grab hold of.

'Nails!' said Nightingale.

'You haven't got time to paint your nails!' screamed Slug Boy. 'Because, I don't know if I mentioned it, but ***I'M STILL GOING TO BE SMASHED TO SMITHEREENS!!***'

'FASTEN YOUR SEATBELT,' shouted Nightingale. **'THERE MIGHT BE SOME TURBULENCE.'**

She dived for the big nails on the back and gripped them as tightly as she could. They were just far enough off the ground for her to let her skis dangle in the snow and she squeezed all her strength into her toes. Her legs became anchors and as she was dragged along, bumping and skidding, digging in with her skis, the hut started to slow. The metal nails were freezing, though, and the pain in her fingers was unbearable.

Luckily, KangaRuby and The Chimp weren't far behind. When the runaway tinklehouzen had rocketed down the slope, they had transformed into their superhero selves too. The first thing KangaRuby did was pull a rocking horse out of her pocket and it proved to be the perfect vehicle: brilliant for sitting on and sliding down the mountain at top speed.

'**HANG ON, NIGHTINGALE!**' shouted the Chimp, who was driving while KangaRuby sat at the back, fishing more things out of her pocket.

The Chimp steered the rocking horse around trees, rocks and pylons.

'Try to find something really heavy,' he called to KangaRuby. 'I reckon the best way to slow it down is to smash it up.'

KangaRuby pulled out a snail, a comb and a tin-opener. None of them very heavy or very useful. Then she took out a pair of pyjamas.

'**PERFECT!**' said The Chimp.

'Are they?' asked a baffled KangaRuby. But The Chimp had got a brilliant idea.

The rocking horse was now neck and neck with the runaway hut, which was just as well, because Nightingale lost her grip on the nails.

'*AAAGGGHH*,' she yelled, her fingers stinging with cold as she crashed into the snow.

KangaRuby took over steering, while The Chimp tied knots in the legs of the pyjamas and held them in the air.

'Keep it steady,' he shouted. 'I'm going to jump.' He leapt towards the tinklehouzen like a cowboy jumping from one stampeding horse to another. 'Gerrrronimo!' he yelled and landed perfectly.

Slug Boy kept his eye to the crack in the tinklehouzen wall. More trees flashed past. More black flags, more rocks and then signs that said,

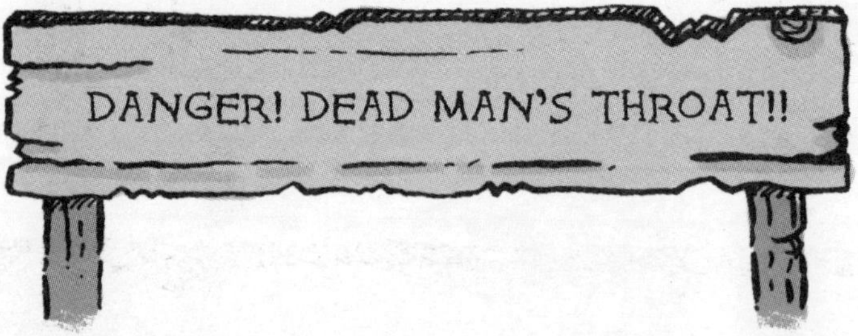

Up ahead was the hole in the mountain they'd been warned about by Mr Kreep. It was like a bite in the rock, a wound caused by an asteroid over 100 million

years before. The asteroid had fallen so hard that people said it plunged all the way to the earth's core.

'Nobody knows how deep it is,' Kreep had hissed. 'It is a hole with no bottom.'

'Better than a bottom with no hole!' joked Morris and everybody had laughed at the time (except Kreep).

Slug Boy wasn't laughing now. More signs flashed past:

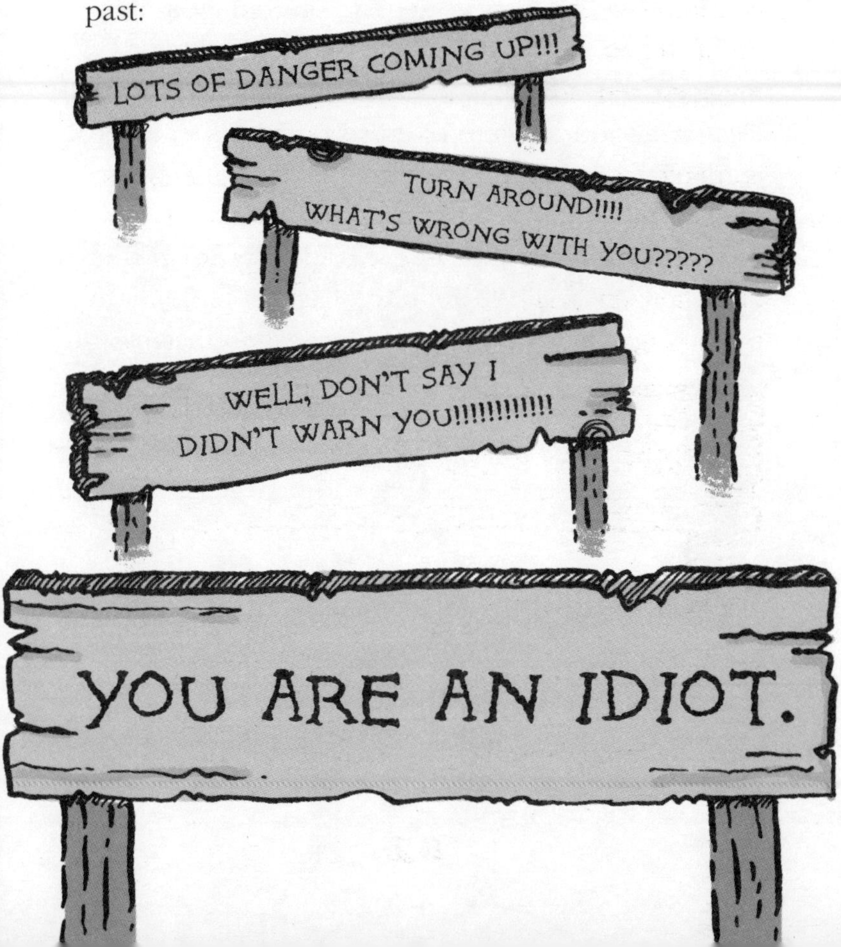

LOTS OF DANGER COMING UP!!!
TURN AROUND!!!!
WHAT'S WRONG WITH YOU?????
WELL, DON'T SAY I
DIDN'T WARN YOU!!!!!!!!!!!!
YOU ARE AN IDIOT.

The little wooden hut was swerving and wobbling, but The Chimp gripped on tightly with his feet. Inside, poor Slug Boy bit his slimy lip. Balancing brilliantly, The Chimp waved the pyjama bottoms high above his head and they filled with air like a parachute. The tinklehouzen started to slow.

'WE'RE GOING TO MAKE IT!' he yelled. **'IT'S THE CHIMP RIDING TO THE RESCUE. YEEEEHAA!'**

But The Chimp was wrong. The hut was going too fast and so was the rocking horse. Both crashed through the safety fence in front of Dead Man's Throat. Wood shattered. Splinters flew. The deep, dark crack in the earth grinned, ready to devour them all.

LANDING LIGHT

One minute, the tinklehouzen and the rocking horse were there. The next, they weren't. It happened so fast it looked like they'd been abducted by aliens or zapped by a wizard.

In the tiny stretch of snow between the safety fence and Dead Man's Throat was an invisible trap door. It was the entrance to a secret tunnel that stretched across the ravine. The tunnel had been built by Grubski so that Bigfoot and Frogurt could move from one side of the mountain to the other without attracting attention. They'd used it on dozens of crooked jobs in the past, like stealing skis and rustling reindeer. Anything in the tunnel was swept along the icy walls, gathering speed, whizzing faster and faster, until it was catapulted out of the other end.

'*YEEEUUUUUGHHHHHHH*,' screamed KangaRuby.

'*WWWWAAAAAAAAAAAAAHH*,' yelled The Chimp.

'*WUUUUUUUUUUUUUUUUUUUUUUUUUUUUUUUUUGH*,' shouted Slug Boy.

The three Fish Fingers fizzed into the sky like torpedoes until gravity did what gravity does and everything that had gone up came plummeting down.

One by one the tinklehouzen, Slug Boy, The Chimp, the rocking horse and KangaRuby fell towards the earth and crashed, smashed and bashed into . . . a giant snowman. To be precise, a giant snowman built by two villainous henchmen, who'd been standing next to it until their unexpected visitors dropped in. Now Bigfoot and Frogurt were lying in the snow, mouths full of slush and heads full of stars. Debris from the tinklehouzen lay scattered across the mountain. Bigfoot had a toilet seat around his neck and a loo brush sticking out of his ear. Frogurt was wrapped up in so much toilet paper he looked like an Egyptian mummy with a very runny nose.

Until then, the villains had been having a lovely day. Mee had led them all over the mountain, trying to follow the scent on Vladi's sock, but she hadn't found a single vampire. (The closest she'd come was a bad-tempered squirrel, but his teeth weren't even pointy.) So Bigfoot and Frogurt had decided to make a snowman with beetroot eyes, a beetroot nose and a curly beetroot chip mouth.

Inside the wreckage of the hut, Slug Boy was groggy and shivering, but alive. He slithered out and couldn't wait to thank his friends.

'**WELL DONE, GUYS!**' he called, but he didn't get much of a reply.

This was because a green, froglike creature was hopping after KangaRuby and a hairy beast with a boot as big as a boulder was chasing after The Chimp. 'That was the bestest snowman we'd ever made!' yelled Bigfoot as he pinned The Chimp to a tree by the scruff of his neck.

'It w-was an a-accident,' protested The Chimp, but Bigfoot picked him up with one hand, planted him headfirst in the snow and swung his great big boot. The Chimp felt a **THWACK!!!** in the seat of his pants and he flew straight into the branches of a prickle tree.

'**UUGGHH**,' he murmured, hanging in the tree like a lost kite.

Meanwhile, Frogurt was catching up with KangaRuby. She was a brilliant bouncer with a head start, but Frogurt could leap higher, further and faster. KangaRuby stopped to grab something from her pocket and it gave Frogurt a chance. He leapt over KangaRuby's head and came flolloping down, squishing the poor little superhero under his belly. 'Got yer!' he laughed, dribbling spittle. KangaRuby wriggled out but she couldn't get up and Frogurt crouched over her face. 'Point one,' he said, 'that snowman was our friend. We named him Gerald.

And you squished him.'

'S-sorry,' said KangaRuby.

'Point two, I do all the leaping about, not you.'

'I didn't mean it,' pleaded KangaRuby.

'Point er, six,' said Frogurt. 'Bigfoot, what's point six again?'

His partner strode over. 'Point six is we don't like uninvited guests. So we have to give them a good **WALLOPING**, a good **WHACKING** and a good **WELLYING!**'

Frogurt smiled and grabbed KangaRuby by the ankles. He twizzled her round, threw her into the air and as she tumbled to earth, Bigfoot swung his terrible toes.

'*YEOOOOOOOOOOOWWW!*' shouted KangaRuby, feeling the force of Bigfoot's big foot and flying towards the same prickle tree that The Chimp was tangled up in.

'Let's get out of here,' said Bigfoot. 'Grubski told us to keep out of trouble.'

'I'm following right in front of you,' said Frogurt.

Sitting on the broken door handle of the tinklehouzen, Slug Boy could only watch as the villains made their escape. The freezing cold had left him stiff as a carrot baton (again), so there was nothing else he could do. Slug Boy saw the fat green one pick up a little pig, which he untied from a tree and then they all jumped aboard a snowmobile and zoomed off into the distance.

It wasn't long before the Fish Fingers were back to normal, superpowers all worn off. Gary and Ruby managed to climb down from the tree and they sat with Morris in the crumpled shell of the tinklehouzen. They felt very lost and alone on the wrong side of the mountain. The sun was going down and it was getting dangerously dark. And where was Bel? Was she okay?

TV DINNER

Back at the lab, Bigfoot and Frogurt sat down with a giant bowl of chips to watch their favourite video. This was a recording of when they were contestants on *Thick as a Brick*, a gameshow searching for the dumbest dummy in Transyldovia. It was hosted by Yugo Furst, a man with silver hair and gold teeth who was normally as cool as a fridge full of cucumbers. But not when he met Bigfoot and Frogurt.

In the video Yugo bounded on with a twinkle in his eye, a spring in his step and a beetroot in his pocket in case he got hungry. He beamed at the audience. 'Hello folks, welcome to the show *where there's nothing tricky* . . .'

'*Unless you're a thicky!*' the audience replied.

'**THAT'S RRRRRRRIGHT!**' shouted Yugo. 'Let's meet our contestants.'

To a fanfare of trumpets, Bigfoot and Frogurt stepped on to the shiny studio floor.

Yugo said, 'Hello to you both! Contestant one, what's your name?

'Hang on, I'm sure I know this . . .' said Bigfoot. 'Do I get a prize if I'm right?'

'Er, we haven't started yet,' said Yugo. 'The answer's on your badge.'

'So it is!' said Bigfoot. 'It's Bigfoot!'

'Same to you, contestant two. What's your name?'

'Is it Bigfoot?' answered Frogurt.

After they'd cleared up that confusion, Yugo asked Bigfoot his quiz question. There was only one per contestant on *Thick as a Brick*. (Any more and the contestants would need a lie down.)

'Mr Bigfoot,' said Yugo. 'Apple pie is a famous pie . . .'

'Yes it is!!' said Bigfoot. 'Have I won?'

'Not yet,' said Yugo. 'I haven't finished. Apple pie is a famous pie, but what famous fruit is inside the pie? Is it a) apple, b) banana or c) onion?'

Bigfoot looked puzzled. 'Can I phone a friend?'

'Of course,' said Yugo.

Bigfoot dialled a number and waited for it to connect. A loud ringing sound filled the studio.

'Hello. Who's that?' said Frogurt, answering his phone.

'It's me, Bigfoot,' said Bigfoot. 'What is. . .'

'***YOU CAN'T PHONE HIM!!!***' yelled Yugo, who was already turning pink. Then he quickly composed himself and grinned at the audience. 'Ha ha ha. These contestants and their jokes, eh? Bigfoot, is there anybody else you'd like to phone?'

'My mum,' said Bigfoot.

'Fine,' nodded Yugo, pretending to smile.

Bigfoot dialled another number. 'Hello, Mum. It's me. No, I don't just call if I want something. Yes, I am wearing a vest. How's your bad knee? Ooh, is it? Still, never mind. Anyway, I'm in a quiz, so I have to go. No, you hang up first! No, you! We'll do it together. One two three. Are you still there? No you hang up. This time. And . . . She's gone.'

'I'm afraid we are running out of time,' said Yugo. 'I need an answer.'

'It's on the tip of my tongue,' said Bigfoot.

'What is?' asked Yugo.

'A bit of beetroot drizzle cake I had for lunch,' replied Bigfoot.

The buzzer sounded.

'I'm sorry, Mr Bigfoot,' said Yugo. 'But the famous fruit in apple pie is in fact, apple. '

Bigfoot couldn't help it. He kicked the nearest thing to him, which was Yugo. The host landed in the lap of a wrestler in the front row who'd nodded off and thought he was being attacked. Without thinking, the wrestler tied Yugo's legs in a granny knot and this made Frogurt laugh so much he drenched the studio lights in spittle. The lights short-circuited and quickly burst into flames.

'Ooh heck,' yelled Frogurt, leaping for cover.

Bigfoot tried to stamp out the fire, but he put his big shoe through the studio floorboards and made a hole so huge all the cameras fell into it. The programme ended as the fire started to spread, the sprinkler system kicked in and the audience ran screaming from the building to escape the inferno.

'It gets better every time we watch it!' said Bigfoot.

'It sure does,' giggled Frogurt. 'I just wish I got to answer the question sometimes. Yugo always asks you. I think I know the answer now.'

Just then Grubski walked in to the lab. 'What do you have to report from the search?' he asked.

'It went perfectly,' answered Bigfoot.

Grubski looked around for the vampire.

'Although we didn't find any vampires,' admitted Bigfoot.

'So we built a snowman,' added Frogurt.

Grubski sighed.

'Fantastic it was too, until it got squished,' said Frogurt. 'By some little guys in masks.'

'Little guys in masks?' said Grubski suspiciously. 'What were they like? How many were there?'

'Well, there was a monkey one and a bouncy one,' said Bigfoot.

'And there might have been a little talking sausage,' said Frogurt. 'So, about seven.'

'That's three, most likely two, as there's no such thing as talking sausages,' said Grubski. 'But two is still too many. They could be superheroes.'

'Didn't seem very super to me,' said Bigfoot.

'Nor me,' said Frogurt. 'We left them hanging about in a prickle tree.'

Grubski didn't like it. He didn't like it at all. He texted his twin.

Grubski smiled a toothless grin and put his phone back in his pocket.

Evil Twin
There may be superheroes in town :-(
Don't panic, my brother We just need to find that vampire fast. Then the future of Transyldovia is in our hands ;-D

HOWLING WOLF

Gary, Ruby and Morris were huddling inside the broken tinklehouzen to shelter.

'**I'VE GOT IT!**' said Ruby. 'We popped out of a tunnel that came from the nice side of the mountain, so if we find the entrance and jump back down the tunnel, we'll be fine!'

So they all got down on their hands and knees and did a finger-tip search for the door but with no luck. This was because Grubski had cleverly invented a trap door that looked like snow and felt like snow. So it didn't matter how carefully they searched with their fingers, they might as well have been hunting for a puddle in a swimming pool. Added to that, it only opened once a day. (Otherwise, Bigfoot and Frogurt would just keep playing in it.) Eventually the children gave up and walked to the edge of Dead Man's Throat, staring down into the huge hole that had no bottom. Too wide to jump across, too deep to climb down. And they couldn't go round it because the rocks were too steep. Gary threw a stone into the depths and nobody heard it land, if it ever did.

They trudged back to shelter in the shell of the tinklehouzen and, as night fell, Morris began to get the jitters.

'I saw a film like this once,' he said. 'Everybody started freezing to death then they ate each other.'

'So it's Fish Fingers for tea,' said Ruby, trying to make him laugh.

'It's not funny,' said Morris grumpily.

'I'm sure a rescue party will be out soon,' said Gary. 'There's nothing to worry about.'

There was a brief silence, then . . .

AWOOOOOOOOOOOOOOOOoo

Something big, somewhere howled.

'W-what was that?' said Morris. 'I-I don't think we're alone.'

AWOOOOOOOOOOOOOOOOOOOOOOOOOOOOOOO

Louder this time, and longer.

'Wolves,' said Morris. 'Brilliant. That's all we need. At least we won't have to eat each other now, because the wolves will get us first.'

'Come on, Morris,' said Ruby. 'We are superheroes! We need to think like superheroes.'

'We're superheroes without superpowers!' said Morris. 'By the time we're superheroes again, we'll be gurgling through some wolf's digestive system.'

Ruby had an idea. 'We should make a big HELP!

sign out of the broken mirror from the tinklehouzen! It'll be shiny, so a rescue party could –'

'It won't be shiny,' said Morris. 'Because you need light to bounce off the mirror. There isn't even a moon tonight. They'll never see us. We'll be stuck here all night.'

'We can't just give up,' said Gary, who was getting cold. He had lost his dragon hat somewhere in the fight and his ears were freezing. Everyone was shivering. They were hungry now too.

Awoooooooooooo oooooooooooooooooooooooooooooooooooooooooooooooo
TINKLEHOUZEN

The howling again. Even louder, even longer. They couldn't tell if it was one big wolf getting closer or two wolves, howling together. The Fish Fingers sat in silence, fearing the worst.

Then Morris remembered, 'I've got some food in my backpack! Has anybody else got any?'

They'd all brought backpacks for the day's skiing and they opened them up. Morris had some cheese and a chocolate donut with sprinkles. Gary had a banana, but he also found his dad's chef's hat – his dad must have sneaked it in before they left Tumchester. Gary put it on and quickly pulled it down over his ears to warm them up. His dad had been right about that hat after all.

Ruby hadn't got any food in her backpack, just her camera.

'Sorry,' she said. 'Not much to nibble on here.'

But as Ruby was putting her camera away, her finger rubbed against a button on the top and the flash went off.

'It's hardly the time for photos,' said Morris grumpily. But it gave Ruby a brilliant idea.

'The mirror, from the tinklehouzen!' she said. 'We can use the flash to make it shine!'

They gathered together as much of the mirror as they could find, Ruby held her camera up, pressed the shutter and it flashed. The light would have been bright anyway but the broken mirror made it dazzling.

'Brilliant!' said Gary.

'Well done, Ruby,' said Morris, wanting to give her a hug but deciding not to because it would have been a bit embarrassing.

As Morris and Gary huddled together to keep warm, Ruby took photo after photo of the mirror and every flash gave them hope – gave them a chance . . . until the battery ran out.

'I'd only just charged it as well,' said Ruby.

'It was worth a try,' said Gary, patting her arm.

'Broken mirrors are always unlucky,' said Morris. 'It was bound not to work.'

But moments later they heard the wonderful sound of a police helicopter. It landed in a flurry of snow and three figures stepped out and raced across the mountain towards them. They were Mrs Pompidoor, a police officer . . . and Bel.

'Thank heavens we've found you,' shouted Mrs Pompidoor, smothering them all in blankets. 'We spotted the flashing light.'

'Come on,' said Chief Viddle. 'Quick as you can. The dark side of the Flugelhorn is a dangerous place at the best of times.'

Bel hugged her friends and they were all overjoyed to be back together.

Once inside the helicopter, the children apologised for putting everybody to a lot of trouble.

'It wasn't our fault, though,' said Gary. He was about to rat on Snoddy and Ferret but Morris interrupted him.

'I got trapped in a tinklehouzen and it sort of fell over and went down one of the black slopes.' He'd decided not to let on about the bullies because they hadn't meant to do it.

'We are really grateful for your help Chief Constable,' said Mrs Pompidoor. 'Because police officers have lots of better things to do.'

'I admit I could have done without it,' answered the Chief. 'We are urgently looking for a priceless pig who's been missing since yesterday.'

'We might be able to help you with that,' said Gary.

'Really?' asked Viddle.

'Yes, we ran into two very nasty villains on the mountain and they were carrying a pig,' said Ruby. 'One of them was fat and green. The other had a beard and a big foot.'

'I think I saw those two yesterday when the pigs landed on our bus!' said Bel.

'Then maybe you can all help me go through some photographs back at the station,' said Viddle. 'If that's okay with Mrs Pompidoor?'

'Of course,' said the headteacher. 'Anything to help the wonderful police officers of Transyldovia.'

Down on the mountain, the terrible howling began again.

'Awoooooooooooooooooooooooooooooo,' shrieked Bigfoot.

'Ahhhhoooooooooooooooooooooo,' screamed Frogurt.

'Let's face it, singing karaoke in the great outdoors is rubbish,' said Bigfoot. 'It's too cold.'

'It wasn't fair of the Doc to ban us from singing at the castle,' said Frogurt. 'He said I sounded like a baboon with backache.'

'And he said I sounded like a turkey with tonsillitis,' said Bigfoot. 'He just doesn't understand music, that's his trouble.'

They packed up their karaoke machine and headed back to Castle Gristle.

UGLY MUGS

Back at the hotel, Bel explained what had happened after she fell off the runaway tinklehouzen.

'I had slush in my ears,' she said. 'And up my nose. It was horrible. I shook it all out and took off to find you but a terrible mist came down and I couldn't see to fly. By the time it was clear, I'd turned back to normal. I told Mrs Pompidoor you were missing, then I finished the interview with Petrov and . . .'

'You finished the interview?' said Gary. 'When we were lost!'

'We could have been frostbitten or wolfbitten!' said Morris.

'Weren't you worried about us?' said Ruby.

'Of course I was,' Bel replied. 'But there was nothing I could do. And Petrov was waiting.'

There was an awkward silence.

Morris shook his head. 'Photos and interviews. It's all a bit silly if you ask me.'

'It would have been bad manners not to finish it,'

said Ruby. 'What else could Bel do?' She gave her friend a hug.

The next day, when the Fish Fingers arrived at police headquarters, they passed Miss Krystal in the corridor. 'Hi guys,' she said.

'Hiya, Miss Krystal!' they answered. 'What are you doing here?'

'Just dropping off some *pain au chocobeetroot* for the officers. They get very hungry chasing crooks so I do a little baking for them. Would you like one?'

She opened a box she was carrying and handed round the little pastries.

'Delicious,' said Morris. 'And if I do say so myself, I am an expert on this sort of thing.'

Miss Krystal smiled. 'Thanks cutie pie,' she said and gave him a kiss on the forehead. It left a red lipstick mouth behind and Morris blushed. He didn't wipe it off though.

'See y'all on the slopes,' said Miss Krystal.

'See you!' they said together.

'I love her pink outfit,' said Bel. 'Sooo glam.'

Chief Viddle took the children to a computer room, gave them the password to log on and explained, 'You're going to see photos of the fifty nastiest supervillains in Transyldovia. We are sure the crooks who took our pig are in there somewhere. Look very carefully. Call me when you find them.'

The police officer went back to her office while the Fish Fingers searched through the photos. They came across some very ugly mugs.

'Look at this one,' said Gary. 'Rubber Band Man. His arms grow so long he can burgle a house without going inside. Currently in prison.'

'Doing a long stretch?' joked Morris. The others laughed but Gary said, 'We need to be serious, Morris.'

'This is a scary one,' said Ruby. 'It's a thief who slithers on the floor and bites the heads off mice. He's The Sssnake.'

'Charming!' quipped Morris and the girls giggled again, but Gary gave his friend a stern look.

'Okay, I'll be serious!' said Morris.

The Fish Fingers learned lots about Transyldovian supervillains, but the two they were looking for weren't there. It was very disappointing. The children sat scratching their heads until Ruby had a brilliant idea. 'Bel can draw them!' she said. 'You know, like artists impressions.'

They found some paper and pencils and they worked as a team, describing to Bel what they remembered. She captured every hair of Bigfoot's face and his beady eyes and Frogurt's wide mouth and warty skin. Bel said, 'It's definitely the two horrid faces I saw in the sky when the bus crashed. UGH!'

Gary called Chief Viddle from down the corridor. 'We didn't have any luck with your photos so Bel drew them,' he said. 'She's brilliant at art. She won the poster competition, *Transport Me to Transyldovia.*'

'Nice poster,' said the Chief. 'I've seen it on the billboards. Okay, show me what you've got.'

Bel held up her drawings.

'That's them,' said Gary.

'Like a photo,' said Ruby. 'Except better!'

'Spot on,' said Morris.

But the Chief just frowned. 'Then it's time for you to go,' she whispered softly. 'You've wasted three hours of my time when I could have been doing proper police work.'

'But what's wrong?' asked Gary. 'They are the villains we saw – it's definitely them!'

'Impossible,' whispered Viddle. 'These two are called Bigfoot and Frogurt. Or, I should say, were called Bigfoot and Frogurt, because they are dead. Maybe you saw some old copies of the Transyldovian Times and thought you'd have a joke with us. Very funny. One of my men will take you to your hotel. And try not to get lost on the mountain again because next time, I might have to arrest you!'

As the children were escorted off the premises Chief Viddle thought back to the last time she saw Bigfoot and Frogurt. It was years before and they'd invented an automatic chip-making machine by putting twelve lawnmowers in a bath and sticking a deep fat fryer underneath. The lawnmowers were supposed to chop up beetroot and then the chips would go down the plughole into the fryer. It was very nearly, almost, quite a good idea. But Bigfoot – the 'brains' of the operation – had made a huge mistake. He put a big on/off button in the middle of the lawnmowers and when he got in the bath to press it, he chopped *himself* into chips. Frogurt packed him in ice and called the emergency services.

When the police, the ambulance and the fire brigade arrived, Frogurt tried to explain just how Bigfoot had got into such a mess. He jumped into the bath shouting, 'This is what the dumb thicky thicko did!' and pressed the big on/off button, just like Bigfoot. So, two dead bodies. Viddle saw it happen.

For some reason the doctor who came to collect the bodies stuck in her mind. She'd seen him that day and then never again. There was something shifty about him, and boy was he ugly, with a round head and hair like the sprouts of a spring onion.

HUGH KREEP

When the Fish Fingers got back to the hotel they were just in time for dinner. They found a copy of the *Transyldovian Times* on every table and there was a photo of Bel's face beaming from the front page. As the children sat down to read the report, they couldn't quite believe what they read.

SUPERSTAR SMILE

Tumchester schoolgirl Bel Singh, is a heroine. It was her brilliant poster that brought her whole class to Transyldovia and when Bel's school bus was hit by flying pigs, she sang to keep everyone's spirits up. 'My friends were very upset,' said Bel. 'So I sang some wonderful songs.' Then as the bus flipped on its roof Bel was thrown outside and she tended to the falling pigs as they bounced in the snow. 'I love little animals,' said Bel. She was later found shivering by the police. Bel is a girl with a lovely warm smile - and a lovely warm heart, too.

'Wow,' said Bel.

'I don't remember you singing,' said Gary.

'Nor do I,' said Ruby.

'If she was singing, I was tap-dancing and playing the bagpipes,' said Morris.

'I know I didn't actually sing,' said Bel. 'Petrov just invented that bit but it doesn't matter. Petrov says it's okay to tell fibs if it makes a good story.'

'It's not okay if it isn't true,' said Ruby. 'Being honest is really important, especially for superheroes!'

'It sounds like you're a little bit jealous,' said Bel.

'Of course I'm –'

Ruby was interrupted by Mrs Pompidoor, who made an announcement.

'First let me congratulate Bel on doing a wonderful interview for the *Transyldovian Times.* Doesn't she look fantabulous on the front page?'

Everybody clapped except for Gary, Morris and Ruby. Bel was so disappointed with her friends she went over to the next table, where the junior cheerleaders were sitting. They were delighted to have Bel sit with them now that she was front page news.

Mrs Pompidoor carried on. 'Tonight, our delightful hotel manager is going to tell us some amazing legends about Transyldovia. His stories might be a bit scary, but don't worry. They are just stories. So, boys and girls, without further fuss, delay or time-wasting. Without fiddling, faddling, fiddle-faddling or anything else to stop the action. Here is the star of our show, the man who puts the 'man' into manager. May I introduce . . .'

'Hugh Kreep,' hissed the manager.

'That's unnecessary,' said Mrs Pompidoor. 'I was just trying to be nice.'

'No, Hugh Kreep,' he said.

'Well, same to you,' replied Mrs Pompidoor.

'Hugh Kreep is me name,' said Hugh Kreep.

'Ah, sorry I see, er Mr Kreep. I didn't realise. Sorry again. Over to you.'

'Thank ye,' hissed the hotel manager.

Ever since they'd checked in, Hugh Kreep had given *everybody* the creeps. He scuttled around like an iguana and had a strange way of knowing if you did something wrong. Once, in the lobby, Gary picked up an apple from a bowl that was supposed to be just for grown-ups. Kreep's back was turned but he still caught Gary. 'Thieving child! I'm telling your headteacher,' he yelled.

'That dude must have eyes in the back of his head,' Gary muttered.

And the strange truth was – he did. Hugh Kreep also had an eye up his nose and one stuck to his knee. Neither of those were very useful, but they were easier to keep secret than the ones in the back of his head. (Kreep grew his hair long so you couldn't see those two and whenever he opened them, he shut them again fast.)

The hotel manager dimmed the lights. Outside a thunderstorm raged and the wind battered the windows like a spirit rattling chains.

'This place needs double-glazing,' said Morris. 'It's not that expensive either. We get tons of adverts pushed through the letter box at home.'

As he sat down to speak, Kreep stared at his audience with wild, unblinking eyes. Luckily the children could only see two of them.

'The first president of Transyldovia was a man named Vladi the Baddie,' said Kreep, flicking out his tongue. 'Even as a boy, Vladi was gruesome. He'd smother his enemies in peanut butter, roll them in worms and lock them in a room full of hungry woodpeckers. And Transyldovian woodpeckers *love* worms and peanut butter. Legend says that one night Vladi was out hunting woodpeckers when he caught a vampire bat by mistake. He took it home and tied it to a chair while he figured out what to do, but then got distracted by a travelling joke-teller knock-knocking at the door. When Vladi came back inside, he sat down without looking and didn't stop screaming till the next day. Soon, the rumours spread that he was a vampire who drank blood.'

'He probably preferred it to beetroot milkshake,' whispered Morris.

'***SHSSSUSH***,' said Mrs Pompidoor, who was quivering with fear in the corner.

Kreep carried on. 'Vladi became the president of Transyldovia. He was a cruel ruler who made the people walk round with thistles in their shoes and eat raw onions for breakfast. They were terrible times.'

'Couldn't have been worse than listening to this claptrap,' said Morris under his breath.

Kreep continued. 'One morning Vladi's terrible secret was discovered by a young maid in his castle. She was dusting in the cellar when she found Vladi, asleep . . . in a coffin. As the girl backed away, Vladi began to stir. The maid hid, but watched as the president cleaned his teeth. She saw his long, sharp fangs and knew this was a clue that he was a vampire.'

'Or that he had a terrible dentist,' whispered Morris.

'**MORRIS!** Is that you again?' said Mrs Pompidoor, who was under a chair.

Kreep ignored the whispering. 'Then Vladi started to shave and the girl saw no reflection in the mirror. This meant he was definitely a vampire and the girl escaped to raise the alarm.

'Bravely, the people of Flugelville marched on the castle to kill Vladi in the traditional way with a stake through his heart. A butcher said he had one but after attacking Vladi for ten minutes he realised a slice of beef is no good for jabbing into vampires. It is too floppy and everyone got covered in gravy. Somebody else said, "Steak is no good, let's try a sausage. At least it's pointier." The sausage idea was no better, so the maid went to the library and checked. It turned out the type of stake they needed was a sharp wooden stick.'

'And councils want to close libraries,' whispered Morris. 'You never know when they are going to come in handy.'

'**MORRIS!!**' yelled Mrs Pompidoor. 'Will you please **SHUUSSHHH!!!**'

Morris shushed.

Kreep carried on. 'At last they put the right stake through Vladi's heart and his dying words were, "Tell my son I'm sorry." Nobody had heard anything about Vladi having a son before, so the villagers hunted everywhere for him. They knocked down most of the castle walls, but no other vampires were ever found.

Everybody agreed that Vladi's last words must have been the crazy mumblings of a lunatic. But nobody knows for sure . . .'

Kreep stopped speaking. None of the children moved. Not even Morris, who had to admit he was now a bit scared. Mrs Pompidoor crept out from under the chair and her hair was standing on end. She started to clap but nobody else joined in.

'Th-thank y-you, Hugh K-Kreep,' she said. 'A-and don't forget, ch-children, it is only a s-story. N-nothing to worry about.'

Kreep raised an eyebrow. (Several eyebrows but you could only see one of them.) 'Aye, just a story,' he said.

That night the Fish Fingers couldn't sleep. Was Mrs Pompidoor right? Was it just a story or had Vladi been a vampire? And not only that . . . was Vladi the Baddie a daddy?

COFFIN UP BLOOD

Since there was a chance superheroes might be in town, Grubski decided to join Bigfoot, Frogurt and Mee the next day as they searched for a vampire 'under a treee'. They took Vladi's sock with them again and Mee sniffed, while Grubski, Bigfoot and Frogurt followed her with spades. Every time the little pig stopped near a tree trunk the others would start digging, but they didn't find so much as a fang or a coffin nail. Mee mostly sniffed out bits of old beetroot that she quickly snacked on.

After nine hours of digging, Frogurt whispered to Bigfoot, 'I've a funny feeling you should never have washed that sock.'

'But it was so pongy,' said Bigfoot. 'It was putting me off my chips.'

That night the mood in the lab was gloomy.

'Even if we find this vampire, won't he be dead?' asked Bigfoot. 'He got buried a long, long, long time ago so he'll be really, really, really dead. Will your finger-shaped machine work on him?'

'A vampire only dies when it's had a stake through its heart,' said Grubski. 'So with any luck this one should just need waking up. If we can find it.'

At that moment Grubski's twin phoned.

'We need to think like Vladi,' said the deep, gravelly voice. 'He wouldn't just hide his son under any old tree. Ask yourself what would he do. But hurry up. The jubilee is in two days. Any more delays and you might as well flush that prophecy down the lavatory.'

Grubski got out the diary. His twin had reminded him of something. He looked again at the exact wording of the prophecy:

> 300 years from my jubilee
> Sniff out a vampire under a treee

The tree had three eees. Grubski had always thought Vladi was just a bad speller, but maybe that wasn't it. The cogs in his giant brain whirred. Wait!

The old Transyldovian spelling of lavatory was lavatreee. It was the only word in the language with three eees! Vladi's son wasn't hidden outside. He was inside, under the plumbing in the castle! That was where Grubski had found the book in the first place.

'**COME ON!**' he shouted to Bigfoot, Frogurt and Mee.

They jumped into the lift and headed down into the subterranean tunnels once more. Grubski took them to the stinking, dripping ancient pipework where he had found the book.

'This is it!' he said, shining a torch. 'We are now under the old lavatory, or should I say lavatreee! I found Vladi's book here in the sewers.' He squinted up the pipe. 'There don't seem to be any vampires blocking up the U-bend, but I think it's a place to start.'

Grubski waved the sock under Mee's nose in the hope that she would pick up a scent, but the little pig didn't even grunt. Bigfoot and Frogurt looked at each other guiltily.

'Maybe it wasn't Vladi's sock after all,' said Grubski.

'Er, I thought that too,' said Bigfoot.

'Me four,' said Frogurt.

Then Grubski had a flash of inspiration. 'Vladi wrote his diary by hand so the book might just have his smell!' He wafted it in front of Mee and her eyes began to dance. She sniffed the pipes, she snorted at the floor, she had picked up a trail!

The little pig dashed off and led them along deep, dark passageways that were even deeper and darker than the deep, dark passageways they went down the last time. She took them this way and that, following the ancient sewage pipes. Thick, brown sludge dripped from the roof and rats scurried under their feet.

'It is freaking me out down here, Doc,' said Bigfoot.

'Me too,' said Frogurt. 'And let's face it, me and Bigfoot are pretty unfreakoutable.'

'Not to mention unterrifrightenable,' added Bigfoot.

'Is unterrifrightenable the same as unfreakoutable?' asked Frogurt.

'I'm not sure,' said Bigfoot 'I'm so freaked out and terrified I don't know what I mean.'

'**SILENCE!**' Grubski yelled and the henchmen put their fingers on their lips.

They had reached a solid stone wall. A dead end. But Mee kept sniffing at it. Grubski held up his torch. 'This wall may be a door disguised as a wall,' he said.

'Or maybe it's a wall disguised as a door,' said Bigfoot.

'Or maybe it's a bag of chips disguised as a wall,' said Frogurt. 'I hope it is anyway.'

Grubski sighed. 'Bigfoot, I need you to give that wall a gentle little kick.'

Bigfoot did as he was asked. He gently tapped the wall with his boot and it smashed the stones like a wrecking ball. The tunnel collapsed and buried them up to their ears in rubble. Once they'd dug themselves out and stopped coughing, they peered through the dust cloud into a small round chamber. There was light inside from flaming torches and a message written on the floor in blood. In Vladi's spidery handwriting, it read:

HERE LIES A VAMPIRE.

They all gulped. Then Grubski said softly, 'Do you know what Vladi the Baddie's dying words were?'

'Yes,' said Frogurt. '*Take that stake out of my heart or you're going to kill meeeeeeeeeeeeeeeeuuuuuuugggghhhhhhhhh . . . euugh . . . ug.*'

Grubski shook his head and took a big, deep breath. 'Not exactly. Vladi's last words were, "Tell my son I'm sorry." Of course, everybody thought he was he was mad because they'd never heard of his son. But I am certain he lies in this secret chamber. It is time for us to raise him from his sleep.'

Bigfoot and Frogurt started to shiver. The room was definitely getting colder.

'I wish I'd put a jumper on,' said Frogurt. 'Or that I had a warm beard like Bigfoot.'

Grubski turned the tiny pages of Vladi's diary until he found what he was looking for.

'To wake the vampire I have to read these words aloud. You must repeat them after me. They are an old Transyldovian prayer to the dead so they will make no sense to you.'

Bigfoot and Frogurt nodded. They were used to things not making any sense to them. The doctor took another deep breath. Then he read the words from the book.

Abum Abear Aburp

Adog Adoo Apoo

Apea Apie Apingpong

Bigfoot and Frogurt repeated every line and, as they finished the last one, the chamber began to shudder. With a **WHOOOOOSH** a slate grey coffin dropped down from the ceiling, as if hanging from invisible wires. It was blood-stained and covered in cobwebs that flew into the air as it hit the floor. Then, slowly, eerily, the lid began to move.

'Rise, rise and be with us,' whispered Grubski. 'You will find villains like you here.'

Bigfoot and Frogurt shuddered.

The stone lid fell to the ground and a long hand, with fingernails that curled like a raven's claw, gripped the side of the coffin. Suddenly a vampire with long fangs and cold, staring eyes sat up and looked around the room.

The vampire turned to face them, his skin ghostly white, his eyes glowing red, his quiff as black as a crow's wing. Then he the uttered words that the souls in the room would never forget.

GOING IN TO BAT

'**Ooh hello**,' said the vampire. 'Look at the muck in here. I can tell nobody's cleaned this place in a verrrrrrry long time. Still nothing that a bit of elbow grease and a feather duster can't fix eh?'

As the vampire climbed out of the coffin, Grubski's brain whirled with confusion. Bigfoot's eyes popped out of his head and Frogurt's jaw dropped.

That's more sewing I am going to have to do when I get back to the lab, thought Grubski as he picked up Bigfoot's eyes and Frogurt's jaw and made some temporary repairs.

'Lovely to see you all,' said the vampire. 'It's always nice to meet new people.'

Grubski, Bigfoot and Frogurt were all a bit surprised by how chirpy the vampire was. They all expected him to be a lot grouchier. Nastier. More evil. But he wasn't. It was as if he'd taken a nap on a Sunday afternoon and been woken by a bluebird singing in a tree. They were also surprised by his pet guinea pig.

'This is Wuffles,' said the vampire, as he held the guinea pig's paw and waved it at everybody. They all waved back. 'But let me introduce myself. I am Terrorski Riski Peski Friski Duski Brewski Vladi, son of Vladi the Baddie. But you can call me Terry. Everyone does. It's short for Terrorski,' said Terry.

Terry definitely wasn't the vampire Grubski was expecting, but he decided to put Terry's strange mood down to a vampire version of jet lag. He had been (un)dead for centuries after all. They led him back to the lab and sat down to discuss things.

'So, how long have I been asleep?' asked Terry.

'About 300 years,' answered the doctor.

'No wonder I feel queasy,' said Terry. 'My mouth's drier than the bottom of a gerbil's foot.'

'I think your father put you in a trance and hid you in the coffin to save you from the villagers who were attacking his castle. I'm afraid your father did not survive that horrible night,' said Grubski.

'I'm not surprised they killed him,' said Terry. 'Daddy was nasty to everybody. And I still don't know why he saved me. I was a complete embarrassment to him – the shameful "family secret".'

'Why did he keep you a secret?' asked Bigfoot.

'Because I couldn't stand the sight of blood,' said Terry. 'Dad said it wasn't good for the family business. He called me a total waste of fangs.'

The others didn't speak for a second while they took it in. A vampire who hated blood. Terry realised they were a little stunned.

'I'm a milk man,' he said. 'I don't mean I do deliveries – ha ha ha. I mean I much prefer dairy products. You know – milk, cheese, butter, yogurt. Oh, what I wouldn't give for a pint of semi-skimmed and one of those yogurts where you fold the corner over.'

'Oh I love those too,' said Frogurt.

'So do I,' said Bigfoot. 'Although me and him are both chip men really. I've got a few in my pocket if you fancy one.' He pulled out some cold chips and offered them to Terry, but he said he wasn't hungry.

Grubski was starting to lose heart.

'Let's leave the blood thing to one side,' he said. 'Did you inherit anything else from your father?'

'Oh yes,' said Terry. 'I'm not too fond of garlic. Makes me feel all giddy.'

Grubski felt like giving up and Terry could sense his disappointment. He had a thought. 'There is one other thing,' said the vampire. 'Just watch this!'

His body became a crackling blur that shrank and then, in his place, was a vampire bat. An evil-looking, snarling, hissing creature. It screeched around the lab and Bigfoot and Frogurt hid under the table. Then it hovered in the air for a second, blurred and crackled again, before it changed back into Terry.

'Just warming up,' said the vampire, as Bigfoot and Frogurt came out of their hiding place. They gave Terry a round of applause. Next the vampire changed into a cloud of black smoke, filling every corner of the room, and Grubski, Bigfoot and Frogurt started to choke.

'Enough, enough,' coughed Grubski. 'You're bringing on my asthma.'

Terry changed back to his normal self.

'Now for my party piece,' he said. 'You'll love this.'

His face changed from its usual happy smile to a sinister grin of pure evil. He walked over to Frogurt, opened his mouth to reveal his long fangs and sank his teeth into the henchman's neck. As Frogurt fainted, Terry wrapped his long cloak around him and they both disappeared. A heavy mist hung in the air.

For the second time that afternoon, Grubski was

too stunned to move. Bigfoot could only blink. Had the vampire been playing with them? Had all that stuff about hating blood been a cruel joke? Bigfoot thought he might never see his friend again and his eyes filled with tears. Suddenly, there was a knock at the door. Grubski, trembling, pulled it open.

'Hello!' said Terry as he walked in with Frogurt, sniggering behind him. 'Had you going there. These fangs are as blunt as a radish. Couldn't puncture a kid's balloon with them. It's all a question of timing. I flap my cloak just as you think you are seeing me take a bite out of someone's neck. Then I do a quick teleport. I can't go too far of course, not France or the moon, but a mile maybe. Pretty good eh?'

Grubski, Bigfoot and Frogurt gave Terry another round of applause.

'Brilliant!' said the doctor, who was starting to feel a lot better. This vampire certainly had potential.

'Now,' said Grubski. 'As I'm sure you can guess, I didn't wake you up just for a bit of entertainment. I will need you to bring terror to Flugelville by doing some hostage-taking and generally scaring the wits out of everybody.'

'I'd like to help,' said Terry. 'Since you've been so nice to me. But I couldn't possibly. Scaring people was my dad's game. I'm a lover, not a frighter. Spread the joy, that's what I say.'

'Okay then, not to worry,' said Grubski. 'The boys can take you up to the kitchen for a snack. I've got some work to do, but drop by when you've had something to eat.'

'Glad there's no hard feelings,' said Terry.

'None at all,' said Grubski. 'Off you go, you must be starving. Leave Wuffles here with me though. I've got some carrots he can have.'

Half an hour later, Bigfoot, Frogurt and Terry came back into the lab.

'That was lovely,' said Terry to Grubski. 'Frogurt got me a yogurt, Bigfoot got me a big . . . er, what has happened to Wuffles?'

Wuffles was sitting in a cage that was connected to hundreds of wires that had sparks jumping from the top.

'Wuffles will come to no harm,' said Grubski. 'As long as you co-operate. If you try to release him, you will fry him. The cage is connected to 20,000 volts of electricity. It will become live the second you touch the bars. And don't try to teleport him out of there because that will fry him too. Only I know how to turn off the electricity, but I won't do it unless you follow my orders.'

Terry broke down in tears. 'My poor Wuffles! How could you do it to the only friend I've had for the last 300 years. You are despicable. Rotten. Worse than my dad!' He started to wail.

'He's taken that quite badly' whispered Frogurt.

'If the Doc needs him to go around taking hostages and scaring people, that's what he's got to do.'

'Yep,' said Bigfoot. 'You can't make an omelette without treading on a few toads.'

'And you can't make toad in the hole either,' said Frogurt.

Terry was still sobbing. He began spluttering, wheezing and sneezing. 'All this is bringing on my allergies,' he said and Grubski gave him a box of tissues. The vampire soon used them up.

'Right, off to bed then Terry,' said Grubski. 'Because tomorrow you'll be going on a little test run, just to make sure our BIG day goes perfectly.'

As poor Terry moped off, Grubski picked up all the snotty tissues and popped them in a test tube. 'Perfect for that bit in the prophecy about a vampire sneeze,' he sniggered.

I.T. HELPDESK

A few miles away, Gary, Bel, Ruby and Morris were hiding in a bush outside police headquarters. They'd made friends again since bickering about Bel's interview and had climbed out of their hotel windows after pretending to be asleep. Since Mee's kidnapping, security at police headquarters had been tightened up. There were extra guards, more alarms, more razor wire and lots of passcodes. The children stared at the barrier by the gate, the moat and all the high towers.

'I'm not sure this is a good idea,' said Morris.

'How else are we going to find out about those two villains?' asked Gary. 'We need to get back on to that police computer. And it's not as if we are committing any crimes. We are only going to go through the archives.'

The others nodded, but they were all worried.

'It wouldn't be so scary if our superpowers had kicked in,' said Bel.

'But that only happens in an emergency,' said

Gary. 'And this isn't one. We are on our own. Which is fine, we are tough enough to do this.'

'It might be an emergency if Chief Viddle is a supervillain in disguise,' said Ruby. 'She wasn't very nice yesterday.'

'I don't think she'd steal her own pig,' said Morris. Then he looked up at the guards in the towers. 'There is no way we are ever going to get in.'

But just then a delivery van arrived. A man in a red cap lent out of the window and pressed an intercom button by the barrier.

'Two hundred flashing blue lights and some top-of-the-range truncheons,' he said. 'Sorry I'm late. Got stuck in the snow.'

'Good to see you Berni,' said the voice on the other end. 'My truncheon is nearly worn out. I need a new one.'

The barrier rose up and the van drove through the gate, except now the back door of the van was slightly open and The Fabulous Four Fish Fingers were hidden inside.

While the police officer on the front desk was signing for the blue lights and the truncheons, Gary, Bel, Ruby and Morris snuck underneath the counter and slipped into the computer room. Luckily there was nobody else about and they logged on using the same password from the day before.

Ruby was the best typer, so she did all the keyboard work. She found the section for *Dead Villains* and typed in the name 'Bigfoot'. Instantly his face filled the screen.

'Ugh!' said Gary. 'That's him. I'd know his beady eyes and beardy beard anywhere.' Ruby clicked with her mouse and Bigfoot's life history came up.

It read:

'Bigfoot McShoe'

ALSO KNOWN AS:

- **Biggie McShoe**
- **Giant Toe McShoe**
- **Super-Size Sandal McShoe**
- **Huge Sock and Shoe McShoe**

His list of crimes ran for page after page. They included the time he tried to blow-dry his beard by strapping himself to the engine of a passenger plane. The blast took every hair off his head (and beard), shredded his clothes and blew him naked on to the runway, where he was arrested for disturbing the pilots when they were busy.

On the last page, there was a note that read: *Bigfoot is now deceased after accidentally chopping himself into chips. (Approximately 21,362 of them).*

'Sounds like he is *well* dead,' said Gary. 'It's not as if he just had a bad cold. Nobody gets better after being chopped into chips. So there is definitely something funny going on.'

The others agreed.

Ruby typed in 'Frogurt'. His face popped up on the screen and Ruby clicked it. The entry was similar to Bigfoot's. It read:

'Frogurt'

ALSO KNOWN AS:

- **Grotty Horrible Slimey Wart Face**
- **The Incredible Spitting Phlegm Bandit**
- **Dave**

Frogurt's crimes included an attempt to steal the flag from the top of Transyldovia's tallest building. He tried to escape by jumping off the roof but even with his rubbery legs, it was too far. Luckily, Frogurt had an umbrella to slow his fall. Unluckily, he forgot to open it. Frogurt hit the ground so hard he swallowed his own feet and broke 205 bones in his body, a Transyldovian record.

On the last page of Frogurt's entry it read: *On the same day his friend Bigfoot chopped himself into chips, so did Frogurt. (Approximately 18,921 of them.)*

'That's another deceased end then,' said Morris, but Ruby noticed something else. As she scrolled down a little further there was a note about the police doctor who arrived at the scene on the day of their accidents. After collecting all the chips and pieces, he simply vanished.

'Crikey on a bikey,' said Ruby. 'Maybe there is an evil scientist behind it all and somehow he has brought Bigfoot and Frogurt back to life.'

Everyone agreed. It seemed to be the only possible explanation.

Suddenly a light came on in the corridor and the Fish Fingers heard voices. They ducked under the tables.

'Berni do you want to see our new computer room?' asked the policeman who'd been on the desk. 'We've just had new wallpaper. Lovely shade of beetroot.'

Gary, Bel and Ruby didn't move.

'Thanks Roni, I'd love to stay,' said the delivery driver. 'But I've got a load of left-handed handcuffs to take over the valley.' The lights in the corridor went off.

'Right,' said Gary. 'We know everything we need to know. Let's get out of here.'

On tiptoes, the Fish Fingers sneaked past the front desk where Roni was busy trying out his new truncheon. He was banging it on the table, swishing it in the air and hitting himself on the knee. 'Ooh, that hurts,' he said as the kids crept by. But just as they got to the main doors, they swished open and the policeman immediately turned round. The Fish Fingers stood facing him.

'Er, hello,' said Gary.

'We've come to see Chief Viddle,' said Morris. 'She told us to be here at ten o'clock.'

'Hey, what, eh?' said the officer. 'How did you, er get in?'

'We just walked in when that van left,' said Morris. 'Is the Chief here?'

'No she's gone home,' said Roni. 'Ten o'clock you say? She must have meant in the morning.'

'Oh really?' said Morris innocently. 'Never mind, our mistake. See you.'

With that, the Fish Fingers walked coolly out through the front door.

'Sometimes Morris you are totes amazeballs,' said Gary.

Morris hadn't the foggiest idea what that meant but he knew it was probably a very good thing to be.

SNOW JOKE

The next day the sun shone, the woodpeckers pecked and the heady perfume of beetroot milkshake filled the air. (Luckily Morris had brought nose plugs.) The children all went to the slopes for lessons with Miss Krystal and it was brilliant fun from start to finish. Snoddy and Ferret kept well away from Morris because they were scared he'd tell Mrs Pompidoor about them and the tinklehouzen. So Morris actually enjoyed himself. Ruby and Gary got even faster on skis and Bel spent more time with the junior cheerleaders, Skyla, Poopsy, Pinkie and Lullabye. They had been so nice when she sat with them in the dining room that Bel was keen to make them new friends. As Bel sat next to Skyla on the chair lift, Skyla said, 'Babe, I just adore your hair. It's like so retro but like so now, you know?'

Bel smiled. None of the Fish Fingers would ever say anything like that. 'Thanks Skyla,' she said. 'I like yours too. Especially with that gorgeous glittery hairband.'

'All the junior cheerleaders have one,' said Skyla. 'You can come shopping with us when we get home. That would be like, so coool.'

'It sounds lovely,' said Bel.

After their last ski lesson of the day, the Fish Street School children all tried to make a long conga line and come down the slope together. Miss Krystal and Mrs Pompidoor were at the front and Morris was at the back. He was doing well until a half-eaten donut fell out of his pocket. Morris tried to catch it but tripped over and crashed headfirst into a bank of snow. As Morris fell, he caught the ski pole of the boy in front (Ferret) who tried to grab the girl next to him (Ruby). Everybody collapsed like tumbling dominoes and the laughter didn't stop until everybody's sides hurt.

All too soon Mrs Pompidoor said, 'Time to head back to the hotel now children. It has been another fantabulous day.'

But, as they all started to leave, Miss Krystal discovered she had lost her mobile phone.

'I wonder if you guys could help me find it,' she said. 'I must have dropped it when our conga collapsed. It's pink with little sparkly bits on the front.'

Skyla whispered to Bel, 'Sounds like a reeeeally cool phone.'

'That's what I thought,' said Bel.

As everybody started sifting through the snow, Miss Krystal noticed that Snoddy was standing just up the mountain in the shadow of a tinklehouzen. He had something sparkly in his hand and he was studying it carefully.

'**YOU, SNODGRASS!**' she snapped. 'Give me that phone. Don't you know how rude it is to look at other people's private things?'

'S-s-sorry. I wasn't,' he said, handing her the phone.

'Have you been checking the text messages? Looking at the numbers?' she demanded.

'No, no, it's locked,' he said.

'But you must have been pressing the buttons to know that it is locked!'

Miss Krystal called Mrs Pompidoor over and told her what had happened.

'I'm very disappointed, Charles,' said the headteacher. 'Any more trouble and you can spend tomorrow night in your room instead of coming to the Beetroot Ball.'

Snoddy definitely didn't want to miss the ball. Pop bands were going to be there, sports stars, the most amazing food and even the President of Transyldovia.

'I really am sorry,' said Snoddy.

'Hmm,' said Mrs Pompidoor.

At that moment in downtown Flugelville, a bat flapped through an open window at the Von Biddle Hat Shop. The owner, Brian Von Biddle, was busy making bobbles and got the fright of his life, especially when the bat started hissing and snarling at him.

'**WAAAAAAAAAA!!! GET OUT!!**' he screamed.

Lightning crackled from the bat's wings and it made a horrid KAAAAAAAAAAAAA KAAAAAAAAAA-ing noise before it blurred and grew into a caped vampire with blood dripping from his fangs.

Grubski had told Terry he'd better make this 'test run' look good or Wuffles would get it. So he had dabbed tomato ketchup on his teeth with a cotton bud and even rubbed baby powder on his face for extra paleness. It was very impressive.

Terry stared into Brian Von Biddle's eyes and shouted fiercely, '**I WANT TO DRINK YOUR MILK. ER, BLOOD.**'

'D-did you say drink my *milk?*' asked Brian.

'No, I said blood. Definitely blood,' said Terry.

'It sounded like milk to me,' said Brian.

'Don't be ridiculous, I'm a vampire, we don't drink milk,' said Terry. 'We only drink blood and that's what I want.'

'**DID YOU HEAR HIM COLIN?**' shouted Brian to his brother who was in the storeroom ironing some

'Made in Transyldovia' labels.

'Clear as a whistle,' said Colin. 'He said milk before he said blood.'

Terry got flustered. 'Oh you mean just then? Ah yes, now I remember. I was going to say, *I want to drink your mil-lion pints of blood.* But I changed my mind halfway through.'

'I haven't got a million pints of blood,' said Brian.

'And that's why I changed my mind. But, just out of interest, have you got much milk in?'

'Couple of bottles,' said Brian. 'Semi-skimmed. We prefer it to the full fat.'

'**AND IT'S A LOT BETTER FOR THE WAISTLINE**,' shouted Colin. '**IT'S IN THE FRIDGE NEXT TO THE YOGURT**.'

'Ooh yogurt as well?' asked Terry.

'Three black cherry and one with fruit in the corner that you fold over. I think that's a strawberry,' said Brian.

'Nice,' said the vampire.

'I must say you do seem to be taking an unusual interest in our dairy goods,' said Brian.

'Just trying to be friendly before I drink your blood,' said Terry.

The vampire gave a terrible scream, sank his teeth into Brian's neck, flicked his cape and then disappeared in a puff of smoke. But only as far as the kitchen. With Brian still in his hand, Terry helped himself to a yogurt from the fridge before vanishing again.

'Sorry, couldn't resist,' he said.

Colin shouted, '**BRIAN! BRIAN!**' but his brother and the vampire had vanished.

BEFORE THE BALL

Word about the vampire soon spread across Transyldovia. The next day at breakfast the Fish Fingers watched a TV news report coming live from the Von Biddle Hat Shop.

'First it flew through the window as a black bat,' the reporter said. 'A bat blacker than midnight, blacker than a bird in an oil slick, blacker than dirt in a grave. Nobody could say this bat wasn't black because it was. Black all over. Except for its teeth, which were white. And its tongue. That was pink. And its eyes. They were a sort of greeny-blue. Then it turned into a caped vampire before biting Brian Von Biddle and disappearing. Hopefully it won't spoil tonight's Beetroot Ball because it should be a great party. Everyone is going to be there. Except Brian Von Biddle.'

The story gave everybody the jitters but nobody wanted to believe it was true. People tried to find reasonable explanations. Maybe Colin Von Biddle had been drinking too much beetroot schnapps and imagined it all. Maybe it wasn't a real vampire, just somebody in fancy dress. Or maybe it was a real vampire who went into the shop to buy a hat and Brian Von Biddle provoked it. He might have given the vampire the wrong change. It didn't mean there was a nasty vampire on the loose, out to drink blood and kidnap innocent people. . . did it? Nobody wanted the story to spoil the Beetroot Ball.

The Fish Fingers didn't know what to believe but they felt sure there was a link between the vampire – real or not – and Bigfoot and Frogurt.

'I don't know if they are in the same gang,' said Bel, 'but I wouldn't be surprised.'

'Birds of a feather flock together,' said Ruby.

'And that goes for jailbirds as well as ones with feathers,' said Morris.

For now the Fish Fingers tried to put it to the back of their minds. The weather had taken a turn for the worse so it was too windy to ski and they spent the day at the hotel, writing postcards, being chased by Hugh Kreep and waiting for the party.

The Beetroot Ball was held at the Flugelville Natural History Museum each year to celebrate the birth of Transyldovia as a united country. After the death of Vladi the Baddie, things didn't improve much for the citizens. Rulers came and went. There was Dicko the Thicko, Bob the Slob, Tilly the Silly and Duncan the Drunken. Not to mention Arty the Farty and Verruca the Puker. They all brought their own problems and soon there was civil war across Transyldovia and the country split in two. It was years before the sides joined together again, when two rival generals shook hands on a battlefield and sat down to sign the Declaration of Peace. Unfortunately, nobody could find a pen and they were a long way from a stationery shop. They did have a beetroot (they were sitting in a beetroot field) so the generals signed their document with the history-making vegetable. The beetroot itself was then pickled for future generations and put in a crystal jar.

This year there was going to be a huge ball because it was exactly 100 years since the signing of the Declaration. It was also 299 years and 364 days since Vladi the Baddie was made president but not many people knew that.

Up in his hotel room, Morris was getting ready and there was something on his mind (quite apart from the vampire, the froggy supervillain, the other supervillain with the big boot and the mad scientist who must have brought them all back from the dead). Morris was thinking about how he'd been frozen stiff whenever he turned into Slug Boy out in the snow.

I need something to keep me warm, he said to himself. *Or I'm no good to the other Fish Fingers and . . . Got it! Fingers! Fingers is the answer!*

He grabbed one of his ski gloves and he cut off one finger. It was perfect slug size. He'd ask Bel to carry it around in the Slugmobile and he could just slither in whenever he became Slug Boy.

'Brilliant, if I do say so myself!' he said so himself.

In his room, Gary was putting the finishing touches to his hair with gel. By the time he'd finished there were so many spikes on his head it looked as if he was half boy, half hedgehog. Two doors down the corridor Ruby was zipping up a dress she had borrowed from her gran. It was made of blue silk and printed with little white woodpeckers, just like the ones in Transyldovia. 'Smashing,' her gran had said every time she wore it.

Bel was putting on her sari when there was a knock at the door. It was Skyla, dressed in the sort of shimmering gown a cartoon princess would wear before a prince carried her off. 'Hey babe,' she said to Bel. 'That Indian dress is like so adooorable.'

'Thanks,' said Bel. 'I'm very *sari* you can't borrow it though!'

'Oh, I don't want to borrow it. Bit jazzy for me,' said Skyla.

'No, I was just saying *sari*, like *sorry*,' said Bel.

'Right,' said Skyla. 'But I still don't know why you're sorry.'

Bel's new friend didn't have a clue about silly jokes, so Bel decided to change the subject. 'Mrs Pompidoor says it's going to be a cold night and we have to walk.'

'I know, it won't be easy in high heels,' said Skyla.

'I'm wearing these,' said Bel as she put on a pair of stout shoes.

'Whoa babe!' said Skyla. 'No you're not! You need sandals for that dress.'

'My feet would freeze,' said Bel.

'Okay,' said Skyla. 'Wear your walking shoes but carry your sandals in your handbag. Change when you get there!'

Bel laughed, 'Why didn't I think of that!' but when she opened her bag the Slugmobile was inside.

'Sorry, I can't after all,' said Bel. 'I promised Morris I'd carry er, something for him and there isn't room.'

'Tell him you forgot or the maid threw it out!' said Skyla. 'No harm in a few fibs for a good cause. And you're a celebrity now, Bel – you were in the newspaper! You need your sandals!'

Bel decided to take Skyla's advice. She put

her gold, strappy sandals in her bag and left the Slugmobile behind. *What could go wrong on a night like this!* she thought.

The children all gathered in the dining room before they left and Mrs Pompidoor made a little speech. 'Ladies and gentlemen, boys and **GAAAAAAAAAAAACHHHOOOOOOO!** girls,' she began. 'Sorry, I seem to have picked up a sniffle.' She wiped her nose and carried on. 'As you know, it is a very special night for the people of Transyldovia and we are very lucky to be guests. It is only because of Bel's wonderful poster that we have tickets.'

Everybody clapped and Bel blushed.

'I would also like to announce that Bel will play a part in the ceremony,' said Mrs Pompidoor. 'I was told to keep it a secret until now for security reasons, but Bel has been chosen to carry the Great Beetroot of Peace into the hall! **AAAACCCCHHHOOOOOO!!**'

Everybody clapped again and even Hugh Kreep, who was listening from the door, nodded his head. Bel was bowled over. *I'm so glad I've got my sandals now!* she thought

Mr Kreep stopped Mrs Pompidoor as they were leaving.

'Have a cup of this tonight,' he said, handing her a bottle of purple medicine. 'It's an old Transyldovian cold cure, guaranteed to stop ye sneezing. By tomorrow ye'll be as right as reindeer.'

'Thank you very much,' said Mrs Pompidoor. She opened the bottle, gave it a sniff and swigged a good mouthful. 'Lovely,' she said, as the medicine lit a warm fire at the back of her throat. 'Quite powerful though, ahem. *Cough cough*. Koooo-wee.'

'You're supposed to mix it with water,' said Kreep. 'And drink one glass every hour until you go to bed.'

'Ah! Thank you,' said Mrs Pompidoor. 'I will.'

THE BALL KICKS OFF

The entrance to the museum was decorated in Transyldovian flags and long lines of bunting with dangly beetroot shapes. There was a huge poster of President Jetski hanging from the roof and a flashing sign that read, *You Can't Beet Transyldovia.* There were pop stars, movie stars and sports stars who waved at the crowds. Yugo Furst the gameshow host was there and so was Petrov from the newspaper.

When the children from Fish Street School arrived they were ushered along the red carpet and dozens of flash bulbs popped as photographers tried to get a picture of Bel. News was out that she had been chosen to carry the Great Beetroot of Peace. Bel smiled and couldn't help enjoying the attention. Once inside, there was time to nibble at the buffet and 'mingle'. All the grown-ups drank champagne except Mrs Pompidoor who wasn't allowed to because of her flu remedy. The children got fizzy beetroot juice in posh glasses. Morris glanced at the faces in the crowd and saw some people he recognised. Hugh Kreep was there, creeping about. Chief Viddle was chatting to Miss Krystal, who was wearing a long, shimmering silver dress. Viddle and Miss Krystal walked over to Mrs Pompidoor, who was delighted to see them.

'Hello Mrs Pompidoor,' said the Chief. 'I think you have met Melodi.'

'Yes, yes lovely to see you Melodi,' answered the headteacher.

'Melodi is the police ski instructor you know,' said the Chief. 'And, although she doesn't talk about it, she also teaches the President!'

'I didn't realise!' said Mrs Pompidoor. 'We are very honoured to have you instructing us.'

'The pleasure is mine,' said Miss Krystal.

'Did you know it was Melodi's idea to have the poster competition?' asked Chief Viddle. 'She suggested it to the President.'

'You're making me blush,' said Miss Krystal. 'I just wanted to give as many kids as I could the chance to see our amazing country.'

Suddenly a man blew a trumpet and announced, 'The President of Transyldovia will be here in seven minutes. Please take your seats.'

Morris took the chance to give Bel the glove-finger slug warmer he'd made.

'It's to stop me freezing solid when I'm Slug Boy,' he said. 'Pop it into the Slugmobile and I can wriggle in if there's an emergency.'

Bel didn't know what to say. She looked down at her gold sandals.

'I'm really sorry Morris, but er, I couldn't find the Slugmobile. I think the maid threw it out.'

'Oh no!' said Morris huffily. 'Well, never mind I suppose. It wasn't your fault.'

Morris headed off to the buffet leaving Bel on her own but Skyla walked past with her gaggle of friends. 'Hey babe,' she said to Bel. 'Those sandals look fab.'

'Thanks,' said Bel. 'Great idea to pop them in my handbag. A shame there wasn't any room for anything else! Catch you later!'

Bel hadn't noticed Morris come back from the buffet table. It had been closed because the President was on his way and Morris overheard Bel's little chat with Skyla. He tapped Bel on the shoulder. 'Did you leave the Slugmobile at the hotel on purpose?' he asked. 'So you'd have room in your bag for your silly shoes?'

Bel looked at him. 'It wasn't . . .' She didn't know what to say. By now Gary and Ruby were listening. Bel nodded guiltily.

'So you fibbed to me,' said Morris. 'Maybe you thought it made a better story. Well, if there's an emergency someone is going to have carry me. And normally when we try that I end up stuck to a window or sploshing about in a puddle. I just hope nothing happens.'

'It won't, don't worry' said Bel. 'I'm sorry, Morris,' she added, but Morris, Gary and Ruby were already walking off.

At the back of the room somebody shouted, '**HERE HE COMES!**' and the guests all stood up as President Jetski sauntered through the hall, flanked by two tough security guards. The President had a big smile and did a lot of waving. He seemed to know everyone. When he passed the children he said, 'Good to have you Tumchester kids here. I see United are top of the league again. Fantastic.' He winked at Miss Krystal and gave a big thumbs up to Chief Viddle.

When he got on stage the crowd clapped and everybody stood to sing the national anthem. Then the President said, 'Thank you all for coming. What a great chance to celebrate the birth of our country. It makes me so proud to be president at this wonderful time.'

Then he gave a speech for the TV cameras about things like jobs and hospitals and taxes.

As he spoke, Bel was led off by a man in a purple uniform. She was taken to a little room that was guarded by soldiers with guns. Then the man in purple took down a sparkly jar from a shelf and said, 'This is the Great Beetroot of Peace. To the people of Transyldovia it is a symbol of friendship, love and fair play. You will be holding history in your hands.'

Bel peered into the jar. She had to admit the little chunk of beetroot didn't look very valuable, but she understood that it was really, really important.

Meanwhile, arriving at the back entrance were two odd-looking waiters. One had warty green skin, hidden by a long beard and sunglasses. The other had a floppy hat and a big bush glued to his foot. He looked a bit like a normal waiter standing next to a shrubbery. Both waiters were smirking.

'Do you remember why we're here?' whispered Frogurt through his long beard. He was very pleased with his disguise because he had always been jealous of Bigfoot's beard.

'Yes,' nodded Bigfoot. 'To keep an eye on the vampire and er . . . there was something else.' Luckily Grubski had given them a note with specific instructions. Bigfoot pulled it out of his pocket.

Don't forget to steal the world's most famous vegetable.

P.S. This is NOT the Tiny Turnip of Timbuktu

P.P.S. OR the Dancing Parsnip of Disco Island.

P.P.P.S. It is THE GREAT BEETROOT OF PEACE

Bigfoot showed the note to Frogurt who nodded wisely, or at least as wisely as he could. In terms of general wiseness this was about as wise as a potato. A potato who was a bit silly and never listened in potato school.

In the inky black sky above was the invisible airship, switched to autopilot and hovering like a huge, scary bat.

HAVING A BALL

President Jetski was just finishing his speech on the stage as Bel, carrying the priceless vegetable, was led to the doors at the back of the hall.

'So it gives me great pleasure,' said President Jetski, 'to introduce the Great Beetroot of Peace.'

There was a fanfare of trumpets and the doors were opened. Bel walked in slowly, carrying the sparkly jar with both hands. To drop it now would be disastrous. A nation would never forgive her.

A golden table had been set on the stage and Bel walked towards it. As she did so the lights in the chandeliers flickered. No one paid much attention except for the two waiters who were standing at the back of the hall. They winked at each other.

The President said, 'Today the beetroot is being carried by Bel Singh, of Fish Street School in Tumchester. Bel painted the . . .'

The lights flickered again. The President paused, then carried on, hesitantly, as Bel put the beetroot on the table.

'Er, Bel painted the wonderful . . . poster for our tourism . . . campaign this year. She . . .' The lights continued to flicker and a freezing wind blew through the hall. Suddenly, the lights went out. Then . . . '**KAAAAAAAAAAAAAAAAA KAAAAAAA KAAAAAAAAAAA KAAAAAAA!**' Something hideous, a creature, was dive-bombing the crowd, screeching, hissing and spitting. The lights came back on. Everybody screamed and stared at the vampire bat that flapped in the air for a second, then blurred into human form. Terry stood on the stage, arms raised, face a sneer. Nobody noticed as Morris, Ruby, Bel and Gary dashed out of the hall.

By now, the President had been pushed under the golden table by one of his bodyguards. The guard shot his pistol at the vampire, but the bullet went through Terry's body and shattered a window. The President tried to come out from under the table, but banged his head and passed out. The jar with the Great Beetroot inside rolled on to the carpet and down the steps of the stage. It trundled all the way to the back of the hall where a smirking waiter standing next to a shrubbery picked it up.

'***NOBODY MOVE,***' yelled the vampire. '***OR YOU WILL PAY WITH YOUR BLOOD!***' Terry swooped over the crowd but as he did, The Fabulous Four Fish Fingers burst through the door.

'**HOLD IT RIGHT THERE**,' said The Chimp.

'Hold what right where?' asked Terry.

'Just creep back to whichever crypt you crept out of,' said KangaRuby.

'I'm not taking orders from you,' said Terry. 'I'm Terry the Terrible and I'm over 300 years old!'

'Why is it that old people always have to tell you their age?' shouted Slug Boy from inside The Chimp's hand. 'My grandad does it all the time.'

The Chimp somersaulted across the floor and landed a brilliant kick to Terry's tummy but as he did so, Slug Boy plopped out of his hand, bounced off a chandelier and fell into a cup of Mrs Pompidoor's cold remedy.

'**UGGGHHH**,' spluttered Slug Boy as he soaked up the medicine and started to feel whoozy.

KangaRuby dipped her hand in her pocket and pulled out a teddy bear ('No good'), a buttercup ('Worse') and a book about puppies ('**AAAGGG!!!**').

Miss Krystal gathered the Fish Street School children around her. 'Huddle in guys!' she shouted. 'He can't harm us if we all stick together.'

KangaRuby tried her pocket again and pulled out a huge bowl of spaghetti carbonara ('**Yes!!!**'). She launched the dish at the vampire and plastered him in pasta. '**That'll teach you!**' shouted KangaRuby, punching the air.

'**UGH! GROSS**,' yelled Terry, slipping on a mushroom and nosediving to the floor. He caught a whiff of garlic in the carbonara sauce and his knees began to buckle. Nightingale saw her chance and soared above the vampire's head, singing, 'Twinkle, twinkle, little star ...'

Nightingale's song shattered the windows, shook the floor and sent chairs and tables flying.

'How I wonder what you are . . .'

But Terry wasn't beaten. He struggled to his feet and approached Miss Krystal and the Fish Street School kids. He grabbed Ferret and opened his mouth, as if to sink his fangs into his neck. '**STAND BACK OR HE'S GOING TO GET IT**,' he shouted.

Ferret wasn't used to being pushed around by somebody bigger than him and his bottom lip began to wibble.

'**Oh no!**' gasped Nightingale.

'**Chuffin' 'eck!**' exclaimed KangaRuby.

But instead of biting Ferret, the vampire morphed into thick, black smoke and spread out over the crowd like a blast of squid ink. For a few moments, nobody could see their fingers in front of their faces, they coughed and spluttered, they bumped into tables and fell over chairs. Then the smoke cleared.

'OOOOOOOOOOOOOHHHHH NOOOOOOO!' screamed Mrs Pompidoor, all her chins wobbling at once. 'THE . . .VAMPIRE'S . . . GOT . . .ALL THE CHILDREN . . .'

The Chimp, Nightingale and KangaRuby stood in stunned silence. The whole class had vanished.

The Chimp was the first to speak. 'They might not be far away yet. Let's try outside.'

'*BUT WHERE'S SLUG BOY?*' shouted Nightingale.

They scanned the room. 'I lost sight of him when he flew out of The Chimp's hand,' said KangaRuby.

'No time to look now,' said The Chimp. 'Come on!' and the superheroes bolted for the door.

In the museum grounds they could see only moonlight and mist until The Chimp spotted something. 'Look!' he said. 'It's Bigfoot and Frogurt!'

The villains were heading for a rope ladder that rose up, up towards nothing but thin air.

'What has Frogurt got in his hand?' asked KangaRuby, bouncing up to see. '**Crikey me, it's . . . The Great Beetroot of Peace!**'

'*STEP AWAY FROM THE BEETROOT!*' shouted The Chimp but the villains ignored him and started climbing the ladder. The Chimp scrambled up after them and Bigfoot swung his boot menacingly. 'Any closer and I'll really put my foot in it!' he snarled. But his boot got tangled up in the rope ladder and, as he tried to pull it out, he lost his grip and fell, grabbing The Chimp on the way down. The two of them hit the ground with a bump. Agile as ever, The Chimp sprang to his feet but Bigfoot was dazed and his head was spinning. KangaRuby dipped into her pocket and pulled out an electric whisk. As Bigfoot tried to get up, she began whisking his beard.

'*YOW YOW YOW YOW!!!*' he cried as the hairs on his chin twisted into curls. Frogurt leapt down to join in the fight, belly-flopping on top of Nightingale with a squuuuurrsh. The Chimp tried pushing him off, but Frogurt laughed in his face and so much spittle came out The Chimp felt like he'd fallen in a bath of sour milk. It was the most disgusting thing that had ever happened to him (and that was saying something because he'd once had his pants swallowed by a Panteater). The Chimp swung his fist at Frogurt, catching him square on the nose. It made a sound like a rhino stamping on a strawberry and Frogurt tumbled along the ground, setting Nightingale free.

KangaRuby was frantically whisking for her life and Bigfoot was begging for mercy, but then the villain had a stroke of luck. The whisk snapped. The hairs on Bigfoot's chin untangled themselves and he caught KangaRuby by the arm.

'**THINK YOU CAN WHISK *MY* WHISKERS DO YOU!**' he yelled and threw her into a nearby prickle bush. (Not quite as prickly as a prickle tree but still pretty prickly.)

Bigfoot and Frogurt decided they'd had enough of superheroes and started scaling the ladder again.

BATTERED FISH FINGERS

The Fish Fingers were too battered and shattered to follow. Nightingale was gasping for breath after getting squished by Frogurt, KangaRuby was stuck in a bush and The Chimp was wiping toxic spittle from his face. Bigfoot quickly climbed the ladder and Frogurt was following when his mind suddenly went blank. It was a bit like those times when you go into a room and you can't quite remember why you went in there. Frogurt wasn't too sure why he was holding a beetroot jar or what he was doing up a ladder. He remembered something about a note from Grubski, but Bigfoot had it in his pocket and Frogurt didn't like to bother him. No, he just knew he was peckish and he'd left his emergency chips in his other trousers. So he took the lid off the beetroot jar and sized up the priceless vegetable.

Down below and out of sight of the crooks, the three Fish Fingers were all returning to normal. Their hour of superpower was up. As Gary, Ruby and Bel stared helplessly into the sky, Frogurt bit into the

beetroot as if it was an apple. As it was, he didn't think much of the taste.

'Bit old and chewy,' he said to himself and tossed it over his shoulder. It flew through the air like a ball thrown for a dog. Ruby saw it fall, she ran, dived, stretched out her fingers and caught it.

'**PHEW**,' she gasped.

Then Frogurt threw the jar over his other shoulder. Fragile – irreparable if shattered – it went hurtling towards the ground.

'**Keeper's!**' shouted Gary, like a goalie diving for a ball. He launched himself forward. The jar was inches from the ground when Gary rolled underneath it and gathered it safely in his arms.

'**GOTCHA!**' he cried.

Then he noticed something green and squidgy stuck to the side. Gary was just pulling it off when Morris staggered, burping and hiccupping, around the corner.

After his fall into Mrs Pompidoor's cold remedy, Morris was feeling rather odd.

'Well, thanks a didddly to you. I don't think sho,' he said.

'Morris, are you okay?' asked Ruby.

'No! You bunch of nooconpaps. Noncompeeps,' he said.

'I think he means nincompoops,' said Bel.

'So do I,' said Morris. 'I've shaved your wives enough times. Nobody cares about shaving my wife.'

'I think he means he's saved our lives,' said Gary.

'And nobody cares about saving his life,' said Ruby.

'What's happened to you Morris?' asked Bel.

'Mrs Poopidoo's cop of cuff stuff,' he said. 'I've been swimmingly in it. That's where I ended myself up.'

Bel knew it was her fault Morris was like this. If only she had packed the Slugmobile. 'I'm so sorry Morris,' she said.

'We're all sorry Morris,' said Ruby and Gary together.

'Noncompurps, the lot of you,' he said. Then he

saw the jar in Gary's hand and the beetroot in Ruby's. 'What haf you got there?' he asked.

'It's the Great Beetroot of Peace,' said Ruby. 'We saved it from the crooks.'

'Look, why don't you take it inside Morris?' said Bel. 'Say you found it. Then you can be the hero. It's the least we can do.'

'Yesh it is,' said Morris. 'Good. Shuper. That's what we'll do.'

'You should have a drink of water first though,' said Ruby. 'Try to clear your head.'

'My head is clear as a duck, thanking you.' said Morris. He took the beetroot in one hand and held the jar in the other. Then he marched off. In completely the wrong direction. The others waited a moment and Morris came marching back, strode past them and headed towards the hall. Just then, Chief Viddle and President Jetski (with a big bruise on his head) ran around the corner. They spotted Morris.

'**GUARDS!**' shouted the President. '**WE'VE FOUND THE GREAT BEETROOT. ARREST THIS BOY!**'

'Eh?' said Morris.

'He's even had a bite out of it,' whispered the Chief. 'Despicable.'

'I peg your garden?' said Morris. 'I mean, big your darden? Er, dig your pardon?'

Sixteen guards, carrying machine guns and

walkie-talkies, instantly surrounded Morris. The Great Beetroot was carefully placed back in the jar and Morris was put in handcuffs.

'**STOP! WAIT! HE HASN'T DONE ANYTHING!**' yelled his friends, but nobody was listening and Morris was frogmarched off into the night.

VIDDLE'S RIDDLES

Chief Viddle sat in her office, just down the corridor from the cell where Morris was being held. It was going to be a very long night for the policewoman. It had already been a long week. First her beloved Mee was pig-napped (and the only suspects were a pair of corpses). Then a local hat seller went missing, a class of foreign children were spirited away by a vampire on live television and there seemed to be miniature superheroes running around the place. Furthermore, the President was in hospital after banging his head. Even furthermore than that, an attempt had been made to steal the Great Beetroot of Peace and, although she'd caught the thief red-handed, Viddle wasn't sure she'd got the right man. The idiot they'd thrown in the cells didn't seem to fit the profile. Especially as he kept kissing people, telling them they were his best friend and saying, 'Shlugs have feelings ashwell you know'.

The Chief had decided to keep the Great Beetroot at police headquarters from now on. At least it would be safe there. She left her office and walked down to Morris's cell, where the guard opened up.

'He says he accidently drank somebody's flu remedy. I sort of believe him. He's still not quite right . . .'

The Chief thanked the guard and strode in. At that point it would have been a lot better if Morris had stayed in his seat. He could have just waved to his visitor. Instead, he staggered over and said, 'Hello Shief Diggle, er . . . Vibble, I mean Chiggle. Can I just shay, I'm very, very, very . . . uuuggghhh.'

Throwing up all over the Chief's best uniform was not the ideal way to make friends.

'Very very shorry,' said Morris, trying to wipe his mess off the Chief's jacket and her mirror sunglasses.

'Leave it, leave it,' Viddle whispered, marching out and slamming the cell door.

As Chief Viddle sat down in her office again there was a phone call. It wasn't a very long phone call and it involved the Chief whispering, 'Yes, yes, yes,' a lot. Then she took off her sunglasses and put her head in her hands until she heard a voice outside. It was Mrs Pompidoor's.

'**I DON'T CARE IF SHE IS BUSY!**' the headteacher was shouting '**I SIMPLY MUST SEE HER**.' Then she burst into the room with Gary, Bel and Ruby.

'Sorry to bother you, Chief Viddle,' said Mrs

Pompidoor. 'But these children have told me they need to see you urgently, in private. I've told them that Morris's actions were foolish. He should not have been anywhere near the Great Beetroot, even if he did drink something he shouldn't. But I don't believe he is a thief and . . . er, you seem to have something dribbling down your uniform.'

'Yes I do,' whispered Chief Viddle. 'It is some of the buffet that Morris had for his tea. It may also be part of his lunch and a bit of his breakfast.'

'Ah,' said Mrs Pompidoor. 'Sorry.'

'Mrs Pompidoor,' said the police officer, 'I have just come off the phone to the President of Transyldovia. He is feeling a lot better, but he says there is an angry mob outside his hospital. They want him to make an example of Morris, a boy from a foreign country who has vandalized the most important vegetable in Transyldovian history. On top of that, the Mayor of Tumchester wants to know where his children are. It is now an international crisis and trade between our two countries has stopped.'

'Chief Viddle!' said Mrs Pompidoor. 'Nobody is more worried about this situation than me. And I wouldn't be here if I wasn't sure that Gary, Bel and Ruby could help.'

The Chief sighed. 'The last time I sat in this office with your pupils they tried to tell me that dead men had stolen my pig. Maybe they are back to spin more lies! Maybe they are in cahoots with the vampire!'

'That would be silly,' said Mrs Pompidoor.

'Fine. I will give them five minutes,' said Chief Viddle. 'This time, their story had better be good!'

'I'll leave them to it,' said Mrs Pompidoor.

Chief Viddle listened carefully to what Gary, Bel and Ruby had to say and after five minutes she sat back in her chair. 'So, let me get it straight,' she said. 'The vampire only missed you because you went outside to give your friend Morris some fresh air after he drank flu remedy. You think the vampire and Bigfoot and Frogurt are somehow in this together. You say that Bigfoot and Frogurt – despite being dead – stole the Great Beetroot of Peace and Morris is a hero because he saved it. You also claim that the dead men have an invisible plane with a ladder that drops from the sky. Frankly, it seems to me you have been watching too many movies. Have you got one piece of hard evidence to back up your story?'

The three Fish Fingers looked at each other blankly. Then Gary shouted, '**Yes! The nose!**'

'The what?' whispered Chief Viddle.

Gary pulled from his pocket the small, green squidgy thing he'd found stuck to the jar of the Great Beetroot. 'Well, I think it's a nose,' he said, passing it to the Chief. 'It came off one of those dastardly dummies. The one called Frogurt.'

Chief Viddle had to admit the snotty thing in her hands did look like Frogurt's nose. But it couldn't be, could it? Viddle had been there when Frogurt chopped himself into chips and she'd personally handed over the bag to the police doctor. So it was impossible. But it was definitely *somebody*'s nose. There was no doubt about that.

The Chief told the children to wait while she took the nose down to the laboratories and her scientists checked the nose's DNA. Sure enough, it was Frogurt's. The scientists found something else too – a little blob of beetroot juice on the end of the nose that had once belonged to the Great Beetroot of Peace.

So those kids were right, thought Viddle. *I don't know how, but two dead men are walking. Not to mention running, stealing pigs and chewing bits of priceless beetroots.*

After telling a delighted Ruby, Gary and Bel that the tests backed up their story, Chief Viddle led the children down to Morris's cell. Morris was sitting in a chair, nursing his very, very sore head. It felt like somebody was digging a motorway between his ears.

'Hello,' he said, weakly.

'You're free to go,' said the Chief.

'Er, wow. Thanks very much,' said Morris.

Bel, Gary and Ruby ran over and gave him a hug.

When Mrs Pompidoor came to collect them she explained they would be staying for at least another week. With the rest of the class missing, the headteacher had no intention of leaving Transyldovia. 'But you must stay in the hotel at all times,' she instructed Gary, Bel, Ruby and Morris. 'Anybody found going on to the mountain or into the town will be in serious trouble. It is far too dangerous.'

GANG OF THREE

The next morning the Fish Fingers had a meeting. Morris had spent a lot of time in prison thinking and he'd kept himself awake half the night doing some more. Now he had come to a decision.

'I don't want to sound horrid,' said Morris. 'But I think one of us is letting the team down.'

'What do you mean Morris?' asked Ruby. 'I don't quite understand.'

'I do,' said Bel. 'He means me.'

'Sorry Bel,' said Morris. 'But if you're in, I'm out. You need to decide if the truth is more important to you than a good story. I don't think superheroes should go around telling fibs and making up things.'

Ruby started to protest, but Gary said, 'I think he's right. Bel needs to decide if she wants to be a supermodel or a superhero. It was her fault Morris ended up in the cough medicine and we might have beaten those villains yesterday if there had been four Fish Fingers on the job, not three.'

Ruby felt herself agreeing. 'Bel, I think all this

being famous has gone to your head.' Bel didn't know what to say. True friends would be happy for her. Skyla wouldn't be so beastly. 'I think you're ganging up on me. Ruby, you're supposed to be my best friend. I didn't write that stuff in the newspaper. I just answered some questions. And I have said sorry about lying to Morris.'

Ruby said, 'If the choice is Morris or you, I have to say Morris. Your heart doesn't seem to be in it at the moment.'

Bel sobbed. 'You're all just jealous because of the attention I've been getting. You wouldn't even be in Transyldovia if it wasn't for my poster.'

She stood up, wiped her eyes and headed back to her room, slamming the door.

At Castle Gristle, Frogurt was choosing a new nose from Grubski's freezer.

There were so many noses, Frogurt couldn't make up his mind: big, small, pointy, hairy, scabby, warty, Roman, squishy, spotty, with a touch of flu, with bogies.

Suddenly a joke came to Frogurt. Normally he couldn't think of anything funny *on purpose*, but he thought this was funny AND clever.

He shouted to Grubski. '**HEY, I've got a joke! Ha ha. I made it up myself. Okay, what am I doing, over here, right now?**'

'Stop picking your nose,' said Grubski. 'And hurry up.'

'**I'm picking my n–no . . . Oh, you've ruined it**,' yelled Frogurt. He grabbed the closest conk and handed it to Grubski.

'I can't stick that on,' said Grubski.

'Why not, Dr Clever Trousers?' said Frogurt. 'Have you forgotten how?'

'No, that's a Brussels sprout,' said Grubski. 'Pick another nose. And keep away from the vegetable section in the freezer. I don't want your grubby hands all over my tea.'

Grubski was checking the prophecy again. The day of Vladi's 300th jubilee had finally arrived and everything needed to be in place before midnight. Seizing the children had been a big step in the right direction. *Time to get busy*, he thought, casting his eye over the book.

Get a class of kids from over the foam
And feed them soup with a dinosaur bone

Grubski went to check on the soup. He'd made it with bones from his dinosaur collection and it was simmering nicely in a cauldron and smelling foul. He instructed Bigfoot to take it down the dungeon,

'I'll bring Frogurt,' he said, 'after he's picked his nose'

Bigfoot gingerly carried the cauldron down to the hostages but they weren't very pleased to see him. Snoddy was banging the bars with a spoon. 'Let us out!' he shouted as Bigfoot walked through the door.

'FREE THE HOSTAGES!' yelled Brian Von Biddle, the man from the hat shop.

'OPEN UP! OPEN UP!' chanted Skyla and the other cheerleaders. Soon everybody was banging on the bars.

'No need to get yourselves in a tizzy,' said Bigfoot. 'Dinner is served.'

'**CLEAR OFF**,' shouted Snoddy. '**WE 'RE NOT HUNGRY**.'

'Er, I'm quite peckish,' said Ferret.

'Well you're in for a treat,' said Bigfoot getting out some bowls and pouring in the grey sloppy mixture with the giant bones sticking out. The hostages didn't think it looked very appetizing.

'Actually,' Ferret said. 'I ate before I came.'

Grubski and Frogurt (with a new nose) marched into the dungeon. The doctor was running over the prophecy in his mind.

Give the kids a nasty wedgie
Then sprinkle their blood on a famous veggie.

After the beetroot fiasco he was one famous veggie down, but his twin would come up with a plan for that. Now was the time for wedgies and a sprinkling of blood.

'Right,' hissed the doctor to the hostages. 'This is what you lot need to do. First, drink your soup. Then Frogurt will give everyone a wedgie and as you struggle with the excruciating pain, you will take off your socks, put thistles in your shoes and dance. It's an old Transyldovian tradition. After five minutes you will be allowed to wash your feet in this luxury foot spa.'

He held up a bucket of cold water.

'**YOU'RE HAVING A LAUGH!**' yelled Snoddy.

'**NO WAY!**' joined in another child, and then another.

'I thought you might say that,' said Grubski. 'But if you don't follow my instructions, you will feel the force of Bigfoot's big foot. He will now demonstrate.'

Bigfoot got a large pineapple out of a cupboard, threw it in the air and kicked it with all his terrible toe-power. The pineapple exploded, skin and juice splattered the dungeon walls and the hostages got the message.

Just to hammer it home though, Bigfoot started kicking all sorts of other fruit and vegetables: pears, potatoes, passion fruit, persimmons, peas (they were tricky) pomegranates and plenty of things that didn't even begin with P. Soon the children were so scared they'd have done anything Grubski asked.

After they'd drunk the ghastly dinosaur bone soup, Frogurt chose Snoddy as his first wedgie victim, pulling the boy's underpants up so high Snoddy could have worn them as a hat.

'**Yeeeeeeeaaaaaaaaaaaaaaggghh**,' he cried and soon the rest of the class were screaming along. Then the hostages all had to take off their socks and Frogurt handed round thistles for their shoes. To help them dance, Grubski played the Transyldovian Top Five. All the songs were by Transyldovia's greatest pop band – The Beetrootles – and they all dealt with the same subject.

1. Can You Feel the Beet?
2. That's What Makes You Beetiful
3. Beet It!
4. Heartbeet
5. Where the Beets Have No Name

After five minutes of dancing, the children were exhausted and the thistles had done their job – their feet looked like they'd been savaged by a pack of kittens. The children bathed their poor tootsies in Grubski's bucket and soon the water was the colour of raspberry jam.

'**PERFECT!**' laughed the evil doctor. 'The prophecy is now so close to fruition I can taste it. And it tastes fruity. Soon there'll be two new presidents in the palace and one of them will be called Grubski. And so will the other. This may cause some confusion with the paperwork. But we can fix that later. **HA HA HA!**'

IT'S A CAVE, MAN

The kidnapping of a class of school kids by a vampire on live TV had sent everybody in Flugelville into a panic. Many people had locked their doors, too frightened to go out. Others had taken to the streets, wearing crosses and carrying garlic to protest. Soon the roads were gridlocked and there were so many beeping horns, angry screams and crying babies it was enough to wake the dead. (The dead who weren't already awake like Bigfoot and Frogurt.)

Bel was in her room, staring gloomily out of the window. The others were in Ruby's room, discussing their next steps.

'If Bigfoot and Frogurt are in the same gang as the vampire, we should try to find *them*,' said Gary. 'They are just the types to leave clues and I know exactly where to look: the first place we met them.'

'The dark side of the Flugelhorn?' asked Morris. 'You're kidding! It's full of wolves and prickle trees. We'll end up eating each other or we'll get frostbite and our fingers will drop off. We'll be the Fish Fingers without any fingers. Is that what you want? No way!'

'I think it's our best chance,' said Gary seriously. 'Our only chance.'

Ruby didn't know which one of her friends to agree with. Usually, she would ask Bel's advice, but that was impossible now. Maybe it was going to be impossible forever. Ruby felt a lump in her throat. She nodded at Gary. They had to go back to the dark side of the mountain.

Half an hour later the Three Fish Fingers were trekking to the spot where they'd crashed through the fence. Gary was carrying the Slugmobile with Morris's slugwarmer inside. The children had sneaked out of the hotel while Mrs Pompidoor was busy filling in 'Children Missing Due to Kidnapping by Vampires' forms for the Transyldovian government. Now Gary, Ruby and Morris stood on the edge of Dead Man's Throat, peering into the deep, dark, bottomless hole.

'My giddy aunt,' said Ruby. 'It feels like I'm staring into outer space.'

'It's horrible,' said Morris. 'One gust of wind, one wrong step and we'd be . . .' He couldn't finish his sentence. It made him shivery just thinking about it.

'Come on,' said Gary. 'We need to find the tunnel.'

They got on their hands and knees and searched in the snow for the invisible trap door they'd fallen through days before. Morris was the first to give up. 'We've had a good try, but there's just no door **HEEEEEEEEEEERRRRRRRRRRE**,' he said as he stood on it, toppled in and disappeared. The others quickly dived after him.

The tunnel twisted and turned and they slid, skidded and slithered before whizzing out the other end in a burst of snow and ice.

They found themselves next to the prickle tree where they'd fought the henchmen. '**Awesome!**' said Gary, seeing his dragon hat hanging from a prickle. He put it on. The tracks of the villains' snowmobile were still just about visible, so the Fish Fingers began to follow them. But walking in the snow was like wading through porridge in concrete shoes.

Poor Morris was soon puffed out. '**I CAN'T GO ON!**' he moaned.

To his relief, Gary stopped up ahead, next to a clump of rocks jutting out from the snow.

'**The tracks run out here!**' Gary called.

The other two caught up and Morris leaned against the rocks to get his breath back. 'End of tracks means end of trek. So we have been on a wild goose **CHAAAAAAAAAAAAAAAAAAAAAASE** . . .' And he was swallowed up by his second secret door of the day.

'He's like our own little door detector isn't he?' giggled Ruby, as she followed behind with Gary.

The children found themselves in a dark cave and grabbed their torches from their backpacks. They could see the cave led to a tunnel with a tiny speck of light at the end and they began walking towards it. Their footsteps echoed off the walls. Nobody said a word but they gulped a lot. Even Gary gulped – and Gary had to be very scared to gulp.

As they got closer to the light they could see a figure. Just a black silhouette at first. An outline. A dark shadow. But then it was unmistakable. The cape, flapping in the breeze. The fangs. The quiff.

Morris screamed. The vampire screamed. Gary and Ruby screamed. By the time that everybody had stopped screaming they all had earache and the Fish Fingers had transformed into superheroes.

The Chimp yelled to KangaRuby. '**QUICK– have you got any garlic in your pocket? They hate that stuff**.'

As KangaRuby started rooting around, Slug Boy shouted to her, '***GARLIC BREAD EVEN? AND CROSSES. A HOT CROSS BUN WOULD DO! ANYTHING!!***'

KangaRuby pulled out two carrots and a unicycle.

'Sorry,' she said.

But The Chimp grabbed the carrots, held them in a cross sign and started riding the unicycle in circles around the vampire. Terry just smiled.

His dad hadn't liked crosses, but he didn't mind them.

Terry's body blurred and turned into a bat, spitting, snarling and doing a lot of '**KAAAAA-KAAAAAAAING**.' The Three Fish Fingers could have done with a song from Nightingale – their most powerful weapon – but there was no chance of that any more. KangaRuby tried to swat the bat with a cello she'd pulled out of her pocket, but the cave suddenly filled with swirling, black smoke. The superheroes began to cough, but when the smoke cleared, Terry was back to his normal self, sitting on a stone and sobbing.

'It's no use,' he wailed. 'I can't fight. I'm too depressed.'

'You kidnapped some innocent kids and you've scared the living daylights out of the whole town,' shouted The Chimp. 'We're taking you in. What do you have to say to that, hey?'

'I did it for my guinea pig!'

There was a pause.

'Nonsense!' said KangaRuby. 'Just put 'em up or I'll hit you with this!' She pulled out a pancake and

a dandelion and wafted them about in a threatening way.

'Go on, hit me,' sniffed Terry, dabbing his eyes with a tissue. 'I don't care. I'll come quietly. Slap me in irons and take me away!'

He held up his hands so they could put him in handcuffs but the Fish Fingers didn't have any. So KangaRuby put her hand in her pocket and pulled out a waste-paper basket.

'Er, stick that on your head and we'll listen to your story,' said The Chimp, 'Then we'll decide what to do with you.'

Terry did as The Chimp said and told them everything. (It was a bit echoey inside the bin but the Fish Fingers heard him well enough.) Terry said that he preferred milk to blood. He showed them how he teleported. He told them about Wuffles, Dr Grubski and Vladi's terrible prophecy.

'So if Grubski follows each step and makes the prophecy come true, everybody in Transyldovia will be turned into a brain-washed zombie?' asked KangaRuby.

'Sounds awful when you put it like that,' said Terry.

The Fish Fingers couldn't believe it.

'It's well bad,' said The Chimp.

'Just horrid,' said KangaRuby.

'And Grubski calls himself a doctor!' said Slug Boy. 'I bet his patients go in with cough and come out in a coffin.'

The Fish Fingers knew Terry must be speaking the truth and KangaRuby carefully lifted the waste-paper basket off his head. 'Don't get upset,' she said. 'When I feel sad, my gran always says, "turn your frown upside down."'

'And my dad always said "turn your scabs into kebabs,"' said Terry. 'But it never really helped.'

The Chimp then said Terry should come back to the hotel so they could work out a plan together. Slug Boy wasn't having it though.

'Trust a vampire!' he said. 'We've only just met him! And he happens to be the only son of Vladi the Baddie, evil ruler and legendary blood-sucking tyrant!!'

Terry nodded. 'It does sound a bit risky.'

'See, even the vampire agrees,' said Slug Boy.

'We haven't got a choice,' said The Chimp. 'The stakes are too high.'

Terry looked at him nervously.

'Oh, sorry,' said The Chimp. 'No pun intended. Just an expression. Come on, we need to act fast. Our friends need us. And so does Transyldovia.'

THE VAMPIRE STRIKES BACK

Terry teleported the Three Fish Fingers back to the hotel and by the time they stood in Gary's room they were back to normal. They decided that if they were going to team up with Terry, they had better reveal their true non-superhero identities.

'Right then,' said Gary. 'Has anyone got any ideas?'

Nobody had. Ruby kept putting her hand up with the beginning of an idea but then putting it down again. Gary scratched his head. Even Morris stared blankly at the wall.

'I don't want to be a butt-in-ski,' said Terry. 'But it sounds like you need a fresh pair of eyes on this. Is there anyone who can help?'

Ruby said, 'There was someone. But we can't rely on her any more.'

Morris added, 'She's doesn't always tell the truth.'

'She let us down,' said Gary.

'Everybody in my family said I let them down,' said Terry. 'Maybe I did. But it didn't make me a bad vampire.'

'You're right,' said Ruby thoughtfully. 'And it doesn't make Bel a bad superhero. Terry, there is someone who might be able to come up with a plan.'

'Somebody we haven't been very nice to,' said Gary.

'And the sooner we say sorry, the better,' said Morris.

'Lovely,' said Terry. 'Now, nobody minds if I have a bath do they? After 300 years in a coffin I'm as mucky as a farmer's welly.'

Ruby knocked on Bel's door and choking back tears, asked her to come into Gary's room. Bel nodded and followed her. They all sat on the bed.

Gary said, 'Bel, we need you. When it's just the three of us, we are like . . . a shark without a fin.'

'Or beard without a chin,' said Ruby.

'Or a leg without a shin,' said Morris.

'Or a Mickey Mouse without a Min?' added Bel. 'You know, Min-*nie* Mouse!' They all laughed. Bel felt like she was home.

'And we're sorry,' said Gary.

'No, *I'm* sorry,' said Bel. 'I've done a lot of thinking today and I know that having superpowers doesn't make you a superhero. More than anything else, you need to care about doing the right thing and if I can't tell the truth to you guys, I don't deserve to be a Fish Finger.'

'You'll always be a Fish Finger,' said Ruby. 'You just went a bit giddy because of all the celebrity stuff.'

Morris added, 'We shouldn't have ganged up on you Bel. We were numpties.'

'So was I,' said Bel. 'But not any more.'

Ruby gave Bel a huge hug. 'You're my best friend,' she said. 'And always will be.'

Their quiet moment was disturbed by loud caterwauling from the bathroom. '*I had a little fishy, his name was Soapy Sam . . .*'

'What on Earth?' said Bel.

'Oh yeah, there's a vampire in the bath,' said Morris. 'Forgot to mention it.'

Then they brought Bel up to speed. They told her all about the prophecy and what would happen if Grubski made it come true.

They had another big think. Bel bit her lip. Ruby chewed her nails. Gary pulled his fingers so they made a clicky sound. Morris searched his suitcase for inspiration and leftover donuts. '**EUREKA!**' shouted Bel and Morris leapt so high he banged his head on the lid of his case and fell in. '**I've got a plan!**' shouted Bel. '**It's risky but** . . .'

The others all gathered round as she explained. It was definitely the best plan they had come up with (as well as the only plan they had come up with.)

'That is well genius!' said Gary.

'We've missed you so much!' said Ruby.

'Er, I'm not sure about this,' said Morris. 'Does it have to be me who sits in a bath of beetroot juice?'

'You can have my water after me!' shouted Terry from the tub.

'No thanks!' shouted Morris.

'Of course it has to be you Mozza,' said Gary.

'But what if it goes wrong? Purple isn't my colour. It isn't anybody's colour.'

Bel said, 'Transyldovians have been dyeing their clothes with beetroot for centuries. So I'm sure it will be okay on skin.'

'Hmmmm,' said Morris. 'You said everything would be okay at the Beetroot Ball and it wasn't.'

A little tear welled in Bel's eye.

'All right, all right,' said Morris. 'Purple it is!'

The Fish Fingers dashed to the supermarket and spent the rest of their holiday money on jars of pickled beetroot. They hauled them back to the hotel and tipped the contents into the bath, then Morris got in. As he soaked, Ruby set about making a large, empty jar look like the one that housed the Great Beetroot of Peace. She made a super fake label and polished the glass so it shone like crystal.

Soon Morris was glowing a sort of radioactive shade of purple. 'This is not a good look for me,' he said as he looked in the mirror.

A short time later, Gary, Bel, Ruby, Morris and Terry were in the ruins of Castle Gristle. They'd planned to just ring the doorbell but since there wasn't actually a door (let alone a bell) it was a bit tricky. There were only crumbling walls and gravestones.

'Er, now what?' asked Morris.

An owl hooted as the freezing wind sliced through their bones and the moon glimmered like a ghost.

'There must be a secret door here somewhere,' said Terry.'

'Okay, let's spread out and search,' said Gary.

Morris didn't budge. He'd already fallen through two hidden doors and got the bruises to show for it.

As the others hunted high and low, Morris kept himself busy by looking at the gravestones.

One said, *Ivor Badkoff: Died of a Chest Infection*, another read, *A. B. Stunger: Killed by a Honey-Making Insect* and a third was, *Polly Tudor-Legoff: Eaten by a Parrot*. The next gravestone was harder to read, so Morris stepped closer. It said: *Stan Dear*.

'Funny it doesn't say how he died,' said Morris. 'Stan Dear . . . there's something odd about that **na–**'

A door sprang out of the earth, catching him on the chin and knocking him into a prickle bush. The door had a bell and a sign that read, *Castle Gristle – Ring for Service*. While Ruby pulled Morris out of the bush, Gary rang the bell. The Fish Fingers were pretty certain that coming face to face with Grubski or his villainous henchmen would trigger their superhero transformations. But what if it didn't? What if the door opened and they were standing there as four normal kids and a vampire?

They could hear whirring machinery and muffled footsteps. The hairs on their necks stood on end. They heard a bolt slide and a key turn in a lock. Gary started to scratch, Ruby started to bounce, Bel began to hover and Morris began to wobble. The door's rusty hinges began to creak. Just in time, The Fish Fingers were normal no more. Nightingale popped Slug Boy into the jar of beetroot juice and the door swung open.

HOUSE PARTY

Slowly, Bigfoot and Frogurt stepped out of the dark doorway and looked their visitors up and down.

'What are you doing out here?' Bigfoot asked Terry.

'Have you been playing in the garden?' said Frogurt.

'I haven't been playing in the garden,' said Terry. 'We have come to offer you a deal.'

'What do you mean *we?*' asked Bigfoot.

'These guys are with me now,' Terry answered. 'And in this jar is the Great Beetroot of Peace. We know Grubski wants it. We will exchange it for Wuffles and the other hostages.'

'I'm sure the doctor will be interested in your offer,' said Bigfoot. 'He was talking about a famous veggie just the other day. You'd better step inside.'

Bigfoot showed them to the lift. 'Take your shoes and socks off before you get in,' said Bigfoot. 'We've just had new carpets fitted downstairs.'

The Fish Fingers (and Terry) did as they were asked and stepped into the lift. The henchmen said they'd take the stairs, as there wasn't enough room for everybody. As the lift went slowly down, Terry warned, 'Remember, Grubski is an evil genius.'

'Be really careful when the doors open, guys,' said The Chimp. 'This dude could have a death ray up his sleeve or a toxic sludge machine in his pocket.'

'Bigfoot and Frogurt are dangerous too,' said Nightingale. 'Even if sometimes it is accidental.'

'So extra, extra, super, extra alert when we step out,' said KangaRuby.

Slug Boy didn't say anything. He just concentrated on bobbing about and looking like a beetroot.

The lift jerked to a stop at the lab, the doors slid back and The Fish Fingers surveyed the scene. Bigfoot, Frogurt and Grubski stood there, smirking. Chief Viddle's pig Mee was moping in a dog basket and Wuffles was nibbling dandelions in his electrified cage. Terry gave Wuffles a wave and the little guinea pig twitched his nose. 'So nice of you to drop by, Terry,' said Grubski. 'And you've brought some new little friends. Why don't you introduce us?'

'Cut the chat,' said the Chimp. 'Hand over the hostages.'

'We'll give you the beetroot,' said KangaRuby.

'Of course,' said Grubski. 'Step inside. Except, you can't because you are now all superglued to the floor.'

The heroes tried to move but they were stuck fast to the bottom of the lift. 'That's why they made us take our shoes off!' said The Chimp. 'Nothing to do with new carpets.' Even Terry found he couldn't teleport out of the glue.

'I added garlic to it,' said Grubski. 'Works a treat!'

The villains started giggling. Bigfoot and Frogurt thought it was the funniest thing they'd seen since Grubski sat on a pan of hot chip fat and set his trousers on fire.

'Superglued floor! Oldest trick in the book! Ha ha ha,' chuckled Bigfoot. 'And people say Frogurt and me are dummies.'

'What's the pig got to do with it?' said Frogurt. 'Do people call her a dummy as well?'

Over in the dog basket, Mee sighed. These two really were the dumbest henchmen she'd ever met.

Ignoring his henchmen, Grubski snatched the beetroot jar from The Chimp. 'What a lovely gift. How kind!' he said. Just what I always wanted!'

Things weren't going well for our heroes but they all knew Slug Boy could save them, so long as the crooks didn't spot him. He could slither out of the beetroot jar as planned, through an air hole in the lid.

'So this is the Great Beetroot of Peace is it?' said Grubski, holding it up to the light. 'With this in my hand, the prophecy will soon . . .'

Just then, Grubski's mobile rang. The Fish Fingers saw the name 'Evil Twin' pop up on the screen.

'Galloping gobstoppers!' whispered KangaRuby to the others. 'Grubski must have a twin brother! I'll bet he's just as ugly and just as despicable.'

'Funny we haven't seen him around,' said The Chimp. 'It's a small town and if he looks anything like this Grubski, he should stick out like a goat in a goldfish bowl.'

'He's probably in disguise,' answered Bel.

'What?' Grubski said into the phone. 'But if you've stolen the Great Beetroot from police headquarters, what the devil have I got? Right, meet me in the airship in five minutes.'

The phone went dead.

Grubski peered into the jar, but all he could see was the outline of a small purple object floating in the liquid. 'Let's get a closer look,' he said and unscrewed the lid.

KangaRuby chewed her nails, The Chimp closed his eyes, Nightingale held her breath and Terry fanged his lip.

Grubski slowly poured the contents of the jar into a bowl. Slug Boy did his best to stay rolled up and for a few seconds he managed it. But he couldn't keep it up and he flopped out into the dish like . . . a slug-sized superhero. Slug Boy opened his eyes and saw three villainous faces staring down at him.

'Er, hello there,' he said. 'Lovely evening for the time of year.'

'**WHAT THE??**' snapped Grubski.

'**IT'S THAT TALKING SAUSAGE I WAS TELLING YOU ABOUT!**' yelled Frogurt. 'See, I told you there was a talking sausage. You didn't believe me. No such thing as a talking sausage, you said. Vivid imagination, you said. Reading too many comics, you said.'

'**IT'S NOT A TALKING SAUSAGE!**' yelled Grubski. 'It's another superhero. An ugly one I admit.'

'Nice place you've got here,' said Slug Boy. 'You must give me the name of your decorator. Sadly, I can't stop.'

He dashed towards the edge of the bowl as fast as he could. Unfortunately, that wasn't very fast. The crooks didn't even notice he was moving.

'**GRAB HIM!**' said Grubski. 'Stick him back in the jar. Then put the jar in the fridge, padlock the fridge, superglue the padlock and eat the key.'

'Right. Will do,' said Bigfoot. 'But I just lost you at the end there. Can you repeat it?'

'Which bit?' replied the doctor.

'Everything after "**IT'S NOT A TALKING SAUSAGE!**"'

'Oh, never mind!' said Grubski. 'Just stick it in the fridge.' Then he hurried off to meet his twin, taking Mee with him. *I'll leave the pig on the airship*, he thought. *She'll make a nice bargaining chip just in case we bump into Viddle.* Grubski returned a few minutes later, clutching a small, wrinkly beetroot in a sparkling jar.

'This is the *real* Great Beetroot of Peace!' he said gleefully. 'Nicked from under police noses by the joint greatest criminal mastermind the world has ever seen. Frogurt, get a grater! Bigfoot, bring that bucket of blood from the dungeon. I'll get the test tube of Terry's old tissues. We've got a prophecy to fulfil.'

Grubski cleared his workbench and followed each step in Vladi's diary like it was a recipe.

Sprinkle their blood on a famous veggie

He read the words out loud as he spooned the contents of the bucket over the Great Beetroot. Then he wiped the historic veg with the tissues he'd got from Terry when he'd been sniffling about Wuffles.

Smother it in the vampire's sneeze,
And grate it up to look like cheese.

He took a silver grater and ran it backwards and forwards over the Great Beetroot until it was just a pile of purple shavings. Finally, he put the gratings in a plastic lunchbox and started to laugh.

'Right, all we have to do now is pop to the Great Flugel Falls and sprinkle this in the water supply.'

Grubski began to gather his things, when he noticed that Bigfoot was yawning and Frogurt's eyelids were drooping.

'Time for a little energy boost, boys,' he said. 'Don't want you falling asleep on the job. Then, for me its everlasting power and for you it's the biggest chip feast in the history of chips.'

'**YES!!**' Bigfoot kicked the air as if he had just scored the winning goal for Henchmen United in the cup final.

'**Chippeee**,' cheered Frogurt, sending a shower of spittle into the air.

'Can you not do that?' said Grubski. 'I don't even know where it's gone.'

'Sorry,' said Frogurt. 'My bad. I'll get a cloth.'

'Just lie down, the pair of you,' said the doctor. 'We don't have much time.'

Bigfoot was first into his cage and Grubski switched on the finger shaped machine and wheeled it over. He pulled the trigger, pumping his henchman with 10,000 volts of electric power. Bigfoot opened his eyes wide and grinned.

Then the doctor wheeled the machine over to Frogurt. But as he did, he slipped on something green and slimy that Frogurt hadn't wiped with a cloth.

'***Youuuuuuuuuughhh!!!!!***' Grubski shouted. He gripped the trigger to stop himself falling and the machine started zapping the floor, blasting the walls, shooting the furniture.

The doctor steadied himself. No harm done. He jabbed the machine into the bolt in Frogurt's neck and a few seconds later, Frogurt too was wide awake.

'Right, next stop the Flugel Falls!' instructed the doctor, picking up the plastic lunchbox with the terrible mixture inside. Smiling cheerily, Grubski and his henchmen set off for the mountain, leaving Terry, KangaRuby, Nightingale and The Chimp superglued to the lift floor and Slug Boy trapped in the fridge. If the Fish Fingers had a hope of stopping this emergency they needed a huge helping hand from someone, somewhere and fast.

Miraculously, they got it. But it wasn't quite what they were expecting.

DEM BONES

A giant claw tore through the floorboards of the lab, shattering, smashing, splintering everything it could reach. A horn jabbed through the bottom of the lift shredding the floor and the superglue with it. Terry and The Fish Fingers tumbled out of the open door.

KangaRuby peered through the gap in the floorboards and blinked in disbelief. Down below she saw that the claw belonged to a T-rex skeleton. The horn was attached to a triceratops. There was a stegosaurus skeleton too, bashing the walls with its tail and even the bones of a pterodactyl swooping by.

'Er, guys,' she said. 'You might want to take a look at this!'

When Grubski had slipped over, his finger-shaped machine had sent 10,000 electric volts through the floorboards and the pipework to the doctor's collection of dinosaur bones in the Great Hall. Now they were all awake and wreaking havoc. Suddenly, the T-rex bit a hole in the wall and chewed through an electric cable. For a few seconds his teeth lit up like candles on a birthday cake and then all the power in the castle went off.

'**Wuffles!**' shouted Terry. Without electricity, the cage was no longer a death trap and Terry dashed over to free his little guinea pig. The door of the fridge hung open too and Slug Boy shouted, '***HELP!!!!***' Nightingale grabbed him just as the giant skull of a brontosaurus burst through the wall. With no lights in the castle it was difficult to see but one thing was clear, the lab was collapsing around them. The rest of the floorboards gave way and they all dropped into the Great Hall, landing with a crrasssshhh on the thick carpet. The scene was like a prehistoric demolition derby. The tyrannosaurus skeleton was grappling with the triceratops skeleton. The stegosaurus was trying to batter its way out by running at the walls. The brontosaurus was trying to chew his way through the ceiling and the pterodactyl had crashed into a chandelier and was desperately trying to untangle itself. They were all missing one or two bones (since they had been used in Grubski's gruesome soup) but it wasn't slowing them down.

'**HOW DO YOU CALM FIVE JUMPY, BONY DINOSAURS?**' yelled KangaRuby above the racket.

'I could sing?' shouted Nightingale.

'Too risky!' answered The Chimp. 'The walls could

crack. We need to keep those dinosaur bones here. Once they're out, they'll run amok.'

'I won't be too loud,' said Nightingale, dodging to her left as the stegosaurus ran past her and crashed its head against a wall again. 'Music is supposed to soothe savage beasts.'

'We don't have much choice!' shouted Slug Boy, now dangling from the Slugmobile on Nightingale's wrist.

Terry spotted the piano in the corner. 'You sing and I'll play,' he screamed to Nightingale above the din. 'I used to be quite good.'

Terry opened up the piano and ran his fingers over the keys as Nightingale sang, '*Doh-ray-mee-fah-so-la-tee-doh-ray-mee*.'

But it just seemed to make the dinosaurs angrier.

'How about this one,' said Terry.

'Sing along with me when you've got the tune. It's a lullaby of my dad's – the one I was singing in the bath, remember!' Terry started and the others soon joined in.

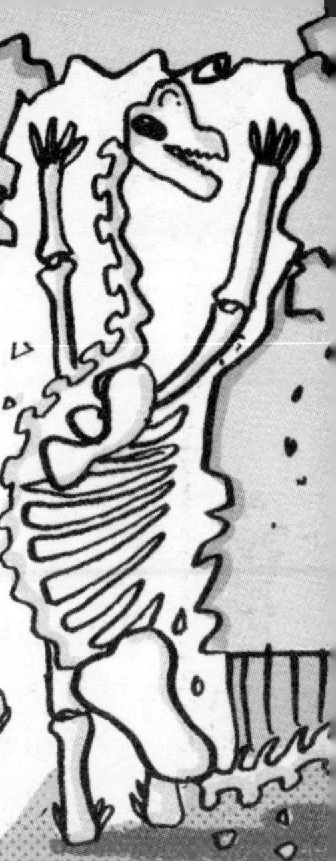

I had a little fishy,
His name was soapy Sam,
He looked just like an onion,
And he smelled a bit like ham.

He liked a game of tennis,
He loved to climb a tree,
But both are very tricky
When you're swimming in
the sea...

Amazingly, it started to do the trick. The dinosaurs all stopped what they were doing, like dazed boxers who'd heard the final bell. They started to plod around the hall, transfixed by the tune. The pterodactyl fluttered to the floor as Terry started again at the beginning.

'That's it, keep going, keep going!' shouted Nightingale.

The dinosaurs were starting to sway in time to the music. The brontosaurus and the stegosaurus even seemed to be wagging their tails. Terry played beautifully and the Fish Fingers sang along in the choruses.

I had a little fishy,
His name was soapy Sam,
He looked just like an onion,
And he smelled a bit like ham.*

The dinosaurs were all much calmer now. The T-rex was rocking gently and the pterodactyl had made a little nest for itself with a tablecloth and some curtains.

'I'll keep singing and playing,' said Terry. 'You go off and be superheroes.'

The Chimp gave Terry a big thumbs-up and the Fish Fingers bounded out of the hall and down the stairs. They followed the cries for 'Help' and soon found the door of the dungeon. KangaRuby pulled a hat stand out of her pocket and the Fish Fingers used it as a battering ram to break down the door.

'**Hallelujah, hallelujah**,' shouted Brian Von Biddle. '**We're saved**.'

'**OMG! OMG!**' yelled Skyla, Poopsy, Pinkie and Lullabye.

* Turn to the back of the book to see Vladi's lullabye in full! Then sing along. Loudly.

'**AWESOME!**' shouted the other children. Even Snoddy and Ferret cried with joy. '**Sick on a brick!**' yelled Ferret as Snoddy patted the superheroes on the back. But as he did, he noticed something familiar about them.

'Aren't you from Tumchester?' Snoddy asked The Chimp.

'Er, yes. No. Sort of,' mumbled The Chimp, trying to disguise his voice. 'We Fish Fingers are citizens of the world. You take care now. And try to be a nicer person,' he added. 'Especially to anyone who is a bit different to you.'

'Even dorks, nerds and losers?' asked Snoddy.

'Yes, even them,' said The Chimp.

Brian Von Biddle was hugging everyone and promising them all free hats.

The Fish Fingers left him to call the police and they raced up the stairs to the front door where they found their trainers. They knew Grubski, Bigfoot and Frogurt would be heading for Transyldovia's biggest waterfall, trying to finish the prophecy, and they dashed off to the mountain to find them.

MOUNTAIN TENSION

Grubski's twin was keeping an eye on things from above in the invisible airship, while the other villains were on a snowmobile heading up the mountain. They had a big head start on the Fish Fingers, but the weather was getting worse – a blizzard was on its way – and it slowed them down.

Bigfoot was driving and bobbing along to the radio. Frogurt and Grubski were playing I-spy in the back.

Frogurt said, 'I spy something beginning with S!'

Grubski replied, 'It's not snow again is it? You've had that every time since we left the castle.'

'No,' said Frogurt. 'It's snowflake.'

'Genius,' said Grubski. 'I'd never have got it.'

Nightingale flew, The Chimp swung, KangaRuby bounced and Slug Boy jiggled about in the Slugmobile as they raced after the villains. Soon they could see them in the distance, the outline of their black snowmobile crawling like a cockroach up the mountain. Nightingale and Slug Boy (snug inside the finger of his glove in the Slugmobile) were the first two superheroes to reach the crooks, just as they got to a clump of prickle trees. Nightingale unleashed a torrent of snowballs she'd been gathering from the high branches. She caught Bigfoot **THUUUUUUNK** on the nose, causing him to swerve and crash into a tree. All three villains tumbled out of the snowmobile. As he picked himself up, Bigfoot snarled, 'You're gonna get the boot now!'

Nightingale carried on bombarding them with freezing missiles.

'*Eeeuuggghh*,' cried Frogurt.

SPLUUURSH went another snowball.

'YAAAAAAAAAAAAAAAAAAAA,' screamed Bigfoot.

THWOK went another.

'GRRRRRRRRRRRRRRRRRRRR,' growled Grubski.

None of the villains could grab Nightingale because she was flying so high and she easily dodged the snowballs they threw back at her. Bigfoot was getting very grumpy and decided to do something sneaky. He whispered to Grubski and Frogurt, 'Keep her busy,' then he hid behind a tree. Bigfoot had decided to take off his shoe, wrap it in snow and make a massive missile out of it. He began pulling at his big boot, but foolishly forgot to undo his laces. Bigfoot tugged so hard his whole leg came off. For a moment he didn't quite know what to do but then decided to make the most of the situation. He rolled his boot *and* his leg in snow. Then when Nightingale was aiming at Frogurt and Grubski, he popped out from behind a tree and launched his leggy snowball.

'Look out!' yelled Slug Boy, but Nightingale turned around too late. **SHMAAAAAASHHH!!** Bigfoot's bigfooted snowball knocked Nightingale out of the sky and she landed face down in a snow drift, dragging the Slugmobile with her.

'I've put my foot in it this time,' laughed Bigfoot. Chuckling and cheering, the villains now circled Nightingale like a wolf pack. She stumbled up and faced them ready for a fight, but Bigfoot's leg hopped behind her and tripped her up. As she picked herself off the floor again, the leg tripped her up again. And again. The villains loved it.

'She's hopping mad now,' laughed Bigfoot.

'I hope she doesn't kick the bucket!' added Grubski.

'Er, what bucket?' asked Frogurt. 'I didn't see a bucket.'

But the villains were too smug, too soon. KangaRuby and The Chimp had arrived.

'Leave her alone,' said The Chimp, grabbing hold of Bigfoot's leg. (The one that wasn't attached to his body.) Bigfoot's leg kicked like a camel but The Chimp wasn't letting go.

'You lot keep turning up like bad smells,' said Bigfoot, hopping about.

'You'd know all about smells,' said The Chimp. 'You're stinkier than a skunk chewing seaweed sandwiches in sweaty socks.'

'Seaweed sandwiches don't wear socks,' said Frogurt.

'The skunks are wearing the socks,' answered The Chimp.

'Oh,' said Frogurt. 'Do we smell that bad?'

'Pongier than a porcupine eating pilchards in a Portaloo,' said The Chimp. 'Whiffier than a walrus . . .'

'**LOOK HERE!**' shouted Frogurt. 'Our whiffs are none of your business.' He leapt into the air and belly flopped towards The Chimp, but the superhero rolled away at the last second. As Frogurt searched under his flabby gut for his victim, The Chimp whacked him from behind with Bigfoot's leg.

'I'm getting a big kick out of you now,' laughed The Chimp.

At last, the Fish Fingers were getting the upper hand (as well as the upper leg). Nightingale was flying rings around Bigfoot, and KangaRuby had Grubski cornered with a bowl of cold rice pudding she'd pulled out of her pocket. It turned out Grubski hated it.

'Keep that away from me,' he shouted. 'Rice has no business being in a pudding. **UGH!!**'

But suddenly the weather turned against the Fish Fingers. The blizzard that had been circling the mountain all afternoon, whipped itself into a frenzy of wind and driving snow.

Nightingale found she couldn't fly against the gale, KangaRuby couldn't bounce either and The Chimp had to hold on to the trunk of a tree to stop himself being blown off the mountain.

After a few minutes, the wind started to drop and the blizzard cleared. KangaRuby, Nightingale and The Chimp rubbed their eyes and as they took in the scene around them their mouths dropped open. The villains had vanished. And so had Slug Boy.

SLUGS AWAY

'Do you think they've kidnapped Slug Boy?' asked KangaRuby.

'Must have,' said The Chimp. 'After all, they kidnapped Mee, a class of school kids and Brian Von Biddle didn't they? They'll kidnap anyone given half a chance.'

'It must have happened when Bigfoot threw his foot at me,' cried Nightingale. 'I was down for a few seconds and they must have grabbed him out of the Slugmobile.'

'Well, at least we know where they're going,' shouted The Chimp. '**The Great Flugel Falls. LET'S GO!**'

Nightingale, The Chimp and KangaRuby raced up the slope like they had jets in their trainers, but the villains were already pulling up at the Flugel Falls. Slug Boy was with them, but he hadn't been slugnapped. When all the others had been fighting on the mountain, Slug Boy had kept very quiet. His superpowers were always at their most superpowerful when people forgot about him and now he was hiding in a dark, cramped space the villains would never guess to look.

The Flugel Falls were about three quarters of the way up the Flugelhorn. Water trickled out of a rock at the top of the mountain like a leaky tap, but soon after the trickle became a brook, the brook became a stream and the stream became the mighty River Dripski. At the Flugel Falls the river dropped over 1,000 feet and Grubski knew the giant waterfall was the key to Vladi's prophecy. It was the source of Transyldovia's drinking water. He knelt down on a ledge that jutted out over the falls, holding the lunchbox full of grated, snotty beetroot and checked the prophecy in Vladi's diary. 'Ah yes,' he said.

Mix it into the city's drinking

And the people won't know what they're thinking

Their brains will be washed: their eyes will be dead,

But they'll think you're the best thing since sliced

. . . beetroot.

'We'll turn every man, woman and child in Transyldovia into a zombie and then they'll thank us for it!!' he sniggered. 'Celebrate boys! This is our moment!'

But it wasn't. It was Slug Boy's.

As Grubski opened the box he noticed there was something in it that hadn't been there when he left the lab: a slug-sized superhero who was busily chomping the horrible gratings.

'Hello again,' shouted Slug Boy. 'It is one of my least well-known superpowers, but I can munch my way through the most disgusting things. This is yummy! Tastes a bit like chicken.'

'**YAAAAAGGGGGHHHHHHHH!!!!**' screamed Grubski. '**WHAT THE . . . ????**'

'We slugs love a bit of rotting vegetation!' chuckled Slug Boy. 'We're famous for it. Now, if you don't mind, pop the lid back on. There's a draft and I'm having my tea.' He munched as quickly as he could, knowing that the future of Transyldovia depended on him. But the plucky superhero had now run out of time.

Grubski shook the box, sending Slug Boy's head into a spin, and he examined the contents closely. Then the scientist sniggered a sigh of relief. 'Lucky for you there's plenty left, you slimy sliver of saliva.'

Bigfoot added, 'Yeah, you stinking sock of spittle.'

Frogurt said, 'Yeah, you ss . . . ss . . . silly sausage.'

Grubski dangled the lunchbox above the rushing torrents of the waterfall again. He threw back his head and started to laugh like a demon who'd just seen his grandmother's wig blow off in a hurricane.

'**HOLD IT, GRUBSKI!**' shouted The Chimp, panting for breath. '**THINK ABOUT WHAT YOU'RE DOING!**'

Nightingale added, 'If you sprinkle that stuff, there is no turning back. Every man, woman and child in Transyldovia will be turned into a . . .'

'**ZOMBIE! YES I KNOW!**' shouted Grubski. '**BRILLIANT ISN'T IT!**' With that, he sprinkled.

The gratings drifted like fluffy dandelion seeds across the waterfall and floated gently into the ripples. The Fish Fingers gasped. And it was definitely one of the biggest gasps they'd ever gasped.

But Grubski wasn't finished. Slug Boy was still clinging to the inside of the lunchbox. 'Just in case your little Sluggy friend coughs up some of the precious beetroot gratings, he can go and pollute the water as well!!'

Grubski shook the sandwich box hard and Slug Boy shot out and flew towards the waterfall.

Not for the first time during his holiday in Transyldovia, Slug Boy yelled, '***HELLLLLL LLLLLLLLLLLLLLLLLLLLLLLLLLPPPPPPPP!!!!!!!!!!!!!***'

THE HILLS ARE ALIVE

As soon as The Chimp saw what Grubski was doing to his best friend, he threw himself towards the waterfall too, but as he reached out for Slug Boy, Nightingale screamed, '**NOOOOOOOOO!**' and rocketed after him.

The Chimp clutched Slug Boy and Nightingale grabbed The Chimp, just before he hit the water. Using every drop of strength in her body, Nightingale somehow hauled her two friends through the air, back towards the mountain.

'You . . . could have drowned,' she panted, but just before she reached the bank, Nightingale's strength deserted her. 'I can't . . . fly . . . any . . .' She plunged into the freezing water, still holding on to the others. As the gushing torrent dragged them down, The Chimp kicked his legs hard. He held Slug Boy in the air with one hand and pushed Nightingale towards the bank with the other.

'**GRAB THE ROCKS!**' he yelled and Nightingale wrapped her icy fingers around dry land. The

Chimp found a crevice too and squeezed his hand inside, but the current was ferocious and he knew he couldn't fight it for long.

'*KANGARUBY! HELP!!*' yelled Slug Boy, still in The Chimp's grip, desperately trying to remember from his library book, *100 Facts About Slugs,* whether or not he could swim.

On the bank, KangaRuby was hunting through her pocket for something – anything – that could help. She pulled out bananas, a trumpet and a cockatoo, then a tin of peaches, a rollerskate, a bird bath, and at last a washing line (complete with washing). She tied one end of the line around a tree and threw the other into the river just as Nightingale and The Chimp were losing their grip.

As the line slapped the water, The Chimp wrapped himself around it like a baby baboon clinging on to its mother's belly. Nightingale grabbed it too and KangaRuby hauled from the other end, screaming 'YOU-CAN-DO IT!! YOU-CAN-DO-IT!!!'

Inch by inch, The Fabulous Four Fish Fingers did do it, and soon they were together again, drenched in sweat and river water, standing on the bank.

As they caught their breath, Grubski interrupted. 'Very entertaining I must say. However, the boys and I have to dash. Our work is done and your screaming seems to have set off an avalanche.'

The Fish Fingers looked up to the top of the Flugelhorn. Sure enough, clouds of snow were billowing near the summit. Then the avalanche started to roar down the mountain. It built from a few white puffs to a colossal inferno of white in seconds.

'Too-da-loo,' said Grubski. 'I don't think we'll meet again but if we do, I'll be President for life, everybody will love me and you'll be arrested immediately. You can try to stop us or you can try to save the lives of all those people down there.'

This time the Fish Fingers stared down the mountain. A pistol shot rang out. It had been fired by Chief Viddle. She was at the head of a large crowd, coming up the slope. There were over 300 people with her – villagers, police officers, mountain rescuers and even Mrs Pompidoor. They were coming to help the Fish Fingers. But they didn't realise they were heading into disaster.

Grubski picked up his mobile phone. 'Quick as you can!' he urged his Evil Twin, who had been hovering overhead in the invisible airship all along.

Seconds later three bungee ropes appeared out of nowhere. Grubski, Bigfoot and Frogurt hooked them on to their trousers and catapulted through the air. BOOOOIIIIIINNNNGGGG!!!! They bounced above the mountain, tied to the bottom of the invisible airship, smirking, ready to be flown to safety.

Someone in the crowd spotted the avalanche and called out. The people started trying to flee but they soon realised they'd never outrun the approaching snow. There was nothing they could do. Soon they would be swept away and so would most of the village.

AVALANCHE!!!!

'**I 'VE GOT IT!**' said KangaRuby. 'Nightingale, I need you to grab my pocket and stretch it right round the mountain. Chimp, you have to hold on to me and wedge us both in to the snow. Slug Boy, you are in charge of cheering us on!'

Nightingale gripped one side of KangaRuby's pocket (it was a lot stretchier than she'd imagined) and flew off faster than she'd ever flown before. The avalanche was closing in, stampeding towards them like a thousand runaway horses. The Chimp held on to KangaRuby as Nightingale pulled and pulled the pocket, stretching, heaving it round the mountain. The avalanche was almost upon them.

Slug Boy yelled, '**HOLD ON!!!!**'

As the snow began to crash around their ears, Nightingale arrived back where she started, with KangaRuby's pocket now wrapped around the mountain. The Chimp put his other arm around Nightingale and gripped her tightly as the avalanche began to swallow them up. But it didn't swallow them up. Instead it dropped harmlessly into KangaRuby's pocket. Her magical, bottomless pocket turned out to be the perfect place to put an avalanche. The Fish Fingers shivered and gripped each other as wave after wave of snow swept down and tumbled inside the deep, deep pocket.

Minutes later, it was over. The sky was blue, the air was clear and in the trees, Transyldovian woodpeckers pecked a joyful peck. The avalanche had passed and the Fish Fingers were alive. Back to normal now, they held each other and smiled. It had been another amazing escape. As they huddled up to keep warm, Gary said, 'Are all those people okay?'

'I think so,' said Bel. 'They are coming this way.'

'And did those crooks escape?' asked Ruby.

'Doesn't make any difference,' said Morris. 'The prophecy is going to come true. The grated beetroot ended up in the water didn't it? So it will be sloshing through all the taps in Transyldovia now. There's no way to stop people drinking it. Grubski won.'

The crowd raced up the mountain to where the four children were huddled. Mrs Pompidoor smothered them in blankets and Brian Von Biddle gave them hats.

'How on earth did you get here?' whispered Chief Viddle. She had plenty more questions for them but this seemed like a good one to start with.

'We were kidnapped,' said Gary.

'By Bigfoot and Frogurt. And an evil mastermind called Grubski,' added Bel.

'And have you seen any superheroes?' said Viddle.

'Er, no. Not really,' said Ruby.

'Well those superheroes have saved the lives of everybody who lives in Flugelville. We owe them a very big thank you,' said Viddle. 'It's just a shame the villains got away.'

'Er, there's something you should know,' said Gary. 'There's this prophecy.'

'Grubski has polluted the water,' said Bel. 'He added some poison to the Great Beetroot and sprinkled it in the Falls. The prophecy says anyone who drinks it will be brainwashed.'

'They'll be like zombies,' said Ruby.

'And they'll think Grubski and his twin are the best things since sliced beetroot,' added Morris. 'I'd say we have all had our chips.'

'There's something you need to know about the Great Beetroot,' said Viddle, but she was interrupted by a shout from the trees.

'**HELP!**' cried Bigfoot.

'**Hellllllllllllllppp!!!!**' yelled Frogurt.

Everybody looked around but it wasn't clear where the shouts were coming from. Then Bel spotted two snowy shapes in the top branches of a prickle tree.

They looked like two giant scoops of vanilla ice-cream.

'Can somebody get us down?' pleaded Bigfoot.

'**We're very sorry!**' shouted Frogurt.

Grubski had escaped without a hitch. His bungee rope had carried him right inside the invisible airship, but Frogurt and Bigfoot had got snagged on a huge prickle tree and, no matter how hard they tried, they couldn't untangle themselves. As the avalanche crashed down the mountain, they got plastered in snow. They were still tied onto their bungee ropes, which seemed to be sticking up like long poles, disappearing into thin air.

As the rescuers began to point and giggle at the dozy duo in the tree, there was a loud spluttering and an explosion in the sky. It was the sound of the engines on the invisible airship. It had been trying to pull Bigfoot and Frogurt out of the prickle trees, but snowflakes from the avalanche had clogged its motors and the engines had overheated. At last they exploded and the airship came crashing to the ground, invisible no longer.

The crowd gasped. Chief Viddle almost ripped the door off its hinges. She dashed inside and the first face she saw was Mee's. The Chief picked up her long lost little pig and they both squeaked with joy.

'I thought I'd never see you again,' she gushed.

Then Viddle approached the cockpit, pistol at the ready but Grubski wasn't looking for a fight. He was cowering under a chair still groggy from the crash.

'It wasn't me,' he lied. 'You've got the wrong man. I only did it because that vampire told me to.'

'We'll track down the vampire later,' replied the Chief, slapping the evil scientist in handcuffs.

The Fish Fingers stepped on board the airship.

'Where's your evil twin brother?' asked Gary. 'He must be here somewhere!'

Grubski didn't say a word.

'He must have been driving the airship!' said Ruby. 'So don't . . .' Her words were cut short by the sound of a door slamming shut and footsteps running off through the snow.

'**That'll be him!**' shouted Bel. '**He must have been hiding. LET'S GET AFTER HIM!**'

They left Grubski handcuffed to a chair and raced outside, but the figure in the snow was well ahead of them.

'Leave this to Mee,' said Viddle. 'Go on girl, fetch!'

The little pig ran like an express train, faster and faster, until she caught up and chomped down hard into the villain's leg. The leg and the villain collapsed in the snow.

'There'll be another medal in this for you!' said the Chief warmly as she patted Mee and stood over Grubski's twin, whose head was buried in a snow drift. The Fish Fingers got there just as the policewoman was about to roll her prisoner over.

'I'm sure it'll be Hugh Kreep!' said Ruby. 'He's just the type and I'm certain he tried to poison Mrs Pompidoor with fake cough mixture!'

But it wasn't the face any of them were expecting.

'Miss Krystal!' exclaimed Gary.

'It can't be,' said Bel.

'But, but, but,' said Ruby.

'I see it now!' said Morris. 'She's his evil twin *sister*! We just assumed it was an evil twin *brother*.'

'That's why she got so cross when she lost her phone that day,' said Gary. 'She didn't want anyone to see who she had been calling.'

Ruby said, 'And at the Beetroot Ball she kept all the children huddled together. Not to save them – to make it easier for Terry to kidnap them!'

– said Miss Krystal, whose real name was Semolina Grubski.

Her voice was deep and gravelly now she didn't have to pretend any more. 'You lot are only here because I persuaded the President to hold that competition. You should be grateful. If it wasn't for me, you'd have never had a holiday.'

'It just shows, pretty on the outside doesn't always mean pretty on the inside,' said Bel.

'We've suspected for a while there was a villain working inside the Transyldovian Police,' said Chief Viddle. 'That's why we laid a little trap. The Great Beetroot of Peace that she stole from HQ today was a fake! We put it there to flush the baddie out. And it did! Our very own ski instructor. So you don't need to worry about the prophecy. The water is fine and fit to drink. By the way, planting a phony beetroot was an idea from our best undercover agent.'

Just then a uniformed police officer brought Bigfoot and Frogurt over. They were handcuffed and foot cuffed (although Bigfoot only had one foot and this made it look like they were in a three-legged race).

'Ah, here's our agent now,' said Viddle. 'I think you might have met him before.'

The agent took his hat off. It was Hugh Kreep. He looked very different in his smart policeman's uniform.

'Hello kids,' he said. 'Sorry I was a bit nasty to you in the hotel. All part of the disguise.'

Chief Viddle said, 'Hugh here is really amazing. Did you know he has got six eyeballs?'

'That's why I became an undercover agent,' said Hugh. 'Having six eyeballs is a bit freaky, but they come in really handy. Or eye-y.'

The Chief asked Hugh Kreep to tuck Mee into bed at police HQ and take all the villains with him.

'You horrible lot are going to prison for a very long time,' she whispered to the crooks. 'Goodbye and good riddance. Now, go with Hugh and Mee.'

'Er, you and who?' said Bigfoot.

'Not me,' answered the Chief. 'I'm staying here. Just go with Mee!'

'You're the Chief of Police,' said Frogurt. 'We have to go with you. It's the law.'

'I'll keep it simple,' said the Chief who grabbed Frogurt by his shirt collar. 'Everybody follow Hugh.'

'Everybody follow me?' said Frogurt. 'But I don't know where I'm going.'

Before the Chief exploded, Detective Kreep dragged Bigfoot, Frogurt and the Grubski twins off down the mountain and Mee trotted behind them.

Mrs Pompidoor appeared.

'I've been looking for you children all over,' she said. 'Come on. We're going to stay in Transyldovia for another week and finally have the holiday we came here for.'

She hugged them and smiled. Even her nasty cold had cleared up thanks to Hugh Kreep's marvellous cough mixture.

FANGS FOR THE MEMORIES

At the Flugelhorn Hotel breakfast began at eight o'clock. But Gary, Bel, Ruby and Morris were up and sneaking out of the door by six. They needed to get back to the castle and find out what had happened to Terry.

Soon they were tiptoeing down the crumbling castle stairs and listening out for the sound of dinosaurs or of Terry playing the piano but there wasn't so much as a foot stomp or a C-sharp. In the Great Hall they found the dinosaur skeletons were just a pile of old bones again. Rubble, dust, stonework, bricks and timber lay over the thick red carpet and although the piano was still in one piece, there was no sign of Terry. But as they turned to go there was a tinkling from inside the piano and their favourite vampire burst out of the lid.

'Look at the muck in here! Don't just stand there. Pick up a duster!' he laughed. 'There's a little peephole! I spied you coming in!'

The Fish Fingers rushed over to hug him and tell

him the villains were all safely locked up and that the town had been saved from his dad's prophecy. Not to mention an avalanche.

'Oh, I'm chuffed to bits,' said Terry.

'But how did you end up in the piano?' asked Bel.

Terry explained that it was midnight before the dinosaurs all went to sleep. 'Those bones could party and it took me ages to wear them out. By midnight we were all frazzled so I settled down for a snooze in here with Wuffles. It was actually quite comfortable – just like a coffin really – and to tell you the truth, I've only just woken up.'

'What are you going to do now?' asked Ruby.

'You need to be careful,' said Morris. 'The police might not believe it when you tell them you're a milk-drinker not a blood-sucker.'

'You can come back to Tumchester with us!' said Ruby. 'You can be the fifth Fish Finger! It'll be brilliant. Go on, go on!'

'What I'd really like to do,' said Terry, 'is go back to sleep in my nice, warm coffin. And what I'd like even more than that is for you guys to tuck me in and say good night. My dad never used to do that.'

So that's what they did. Terry led them down the secret passageway to the chamber where his coffin had been lying for the last 300 years. He snuggled down inside and they all gave him a proper good-night hug.

'It's been well cool meeting you, Terry. You're awesome,' said Gary.

'Sleep tight,' said Bel.

'Don't let the bed bugs bite,' said Ruby.

'And don't bite *them* either,' said Morris. 'Remember you're a vegetarian.'

'Can you say good night to Wuffles aswell?' asked Terry.

'Of course,' they all said together and gave Wuffles a good-night kiss on the nose.

Then they tucked him in next to Terry and put the lid on the coffin. It rose into the ceiling as if on invisible wires and, with tears in their eyes, the children waved it goodbye.

PARTY PARTY

For the next week all the kids from Fish Street School had a ball on and off the slopes. In the evening of the last day there was a party at Flugelville Natural History Museum and the guests included Chief Viddle, Mee, the Von Biddle brothers, Wilbert the bus driver (fully recovered) and President Jetski. The Great Beetroot of Peace was put on display in a glass case and so were the dinosaur bones from Castle Gristle, all stuck back together again. There was a huge banquet, a disco and President Jetski gave Mee a medal.

'It has been the trip of a lifetime hasn't it?' said Gary, as he stood with the others in the main exhibition room. 'But I'm ready to go home now.'

'Me too,' said Morris. 'Transport me to Tumchester.'

'I still can't get over Miss Krystal being so nasty and Hugh Kreep being so nice,' said Bel.

'I'm going to miss Terry,' said Ruby. 'I'll never forget him. I hope he's having sweet dreams of cottage cheese and milkshakes.'

They clinked their glasses to toast the vampire and started singing the song he'd taught them.

I had a little fishy,
His name was Soapy Sam,
He looked just like an onion
And he smelt a bit like ham.

Nobody noticed but as they sang, the skeleton of a huge Tyrannosaurus rex behind them started swaying in time to the music too.

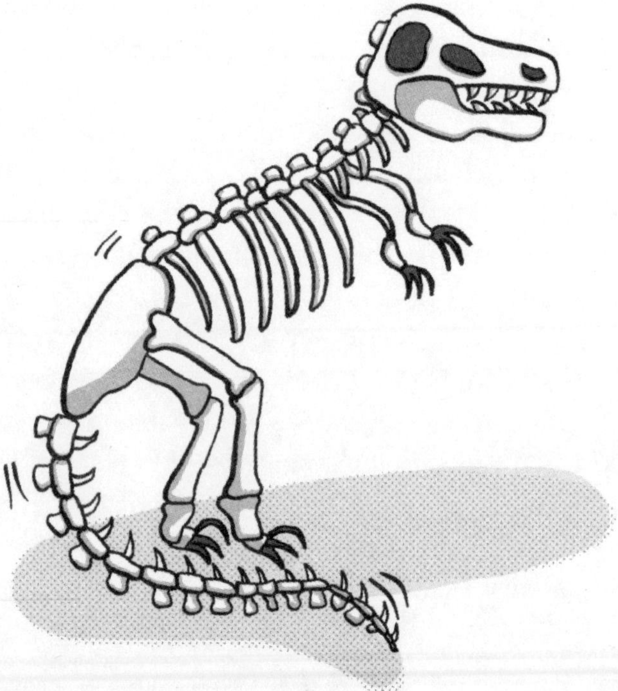

VLADI THE BADDIE'S LULLABY:

I had a little fishy,
His name was soapy Sam,
He looked just like an onion,
And he smelled a bit like ham.

He liked a game of tennis,
He loved to climb a tree,
But both are very tricky
When you're swimming in the sea...

I had a little fishy,
His name was soapy Sam,
He looked just like an onion,
And he smelled a bit like ham.

He liked to fly in rockets,
He loved to drive a car,
But when you're a little fishy
You don't get very far.

I had a little fishy,
His name was soapy Sam,
He looked just like an onion,
And he smelled a bit like ham.

He liked to run up mountains,
He loved to ride a horse,
But nothing's ever easy
When you're a fish of course.

I had a little fishy,
His name was soapy Sam,
He looked just like an onion,
And he smelled a bit like ham.

He liked to jump from aeroplanes,
He loved to sail on ships,
But one day he went missing
Cos my mum ate him with chips.

ACKNOWLEDGEMENTS

In the acknowledgements section of my first book I took the chance to thank lots of people. Many gave me advice, some gave me inspiration, others gave me encouragement. Unfortunately none gave me cash, which was a shame because I need a new car.

Those same people have been lovely all over again but I was told to thin this section down to help save the rainforests so apologies if you didn't make the cut! You are only in this time if you helped specifically or dressed up as KangaRuby on World Book Day (nice one Julie!)

These are the grown-ups:
Roger & Anne Beresford, Kathryn Ross, Liz Bankes, Mark Cameron, Kev & Sue McCarthy, Lara & James Routh, Richard & Wendy Askam, David & Louisa Williams, Mark Barnsley, Dorota Mokszanska, Tony & Suzanne Sharkey, Helen Spencer & Steve Drayton, Michael Ward, Mark & Gabby Nickson, Bill & Amanda Finch, Jim Brassil, Sonny & Dawn Hanley, Jon Doyle, Alfie Hosker, John, Margaret, Shane & Louisa Merrick, Noel Curry, Geoff Foster, Ian Moore, Mark Jones, Carl 'Shaves at Night' Sawyer,

Dave Whitehouse, Chris Twigger, Paul Gilbert, Julie Colley, Wilbert Walsh, Lesley Pendergest, Ian Young, Richard & Fran Hannan, Richard Marsden, Brendon & Leah Guildford, Bill Haw, Marvyn Dickinson, Mark Robinson, Tom Richardson, Andy Beckett, Kerry Allison, Stuart Ramsay, Carolyn Nichol, Phil Crabb, Sarah Hunt, Rowan Homan, Sarah Werkman, Sean Mohan, Nela Willis, Kim Lindsay, Dot Staunton, John Clayton, Sian Williams & Paul Woolwich, Sunita Shroff, Aunty Gladys, Richard, Ellen, Ashley, Chris & Gemma Beresford, Andy & Roz Beresford

These are the kids:
Kitty & Jack Williams, Karl & Jodie McCarthy, Brooke Allison, Mitchell Sharkey, Jamie Hannan, Storm Hanley, Seth & Eve Woolwich-Williams, Sean & Sam Brassil, Fergal & Niamh Curry, Henry Haw, Seamus Mohan, Merlin & Dylan Owen, Niamh, Grace & Erin Merrick, Josh & Izzy Beresford .

And all the staff and pupils of Highfield Primary School in Leeds.

But the hugest, hugest, hugest thanks of all go to my two lovely daughters Laura and Hayley.

FIND OUT HOW IT ALL BEGAN FOR GARY, BEL, RUBY AND MORRIS IN THEIR FIRST ADVENTURE . . .

After a magical, crisp-loving elf turns them into superheroes, **The Chimp**, **Nightingale**, **KangaRuby** and **Slug Boy** must rescue Tumchester from a pair of super-scary and super-hairy villains. But first the **Fabulous Four Fish Fingers** must learn to work as a team (and remember not to step on Slug Boy).

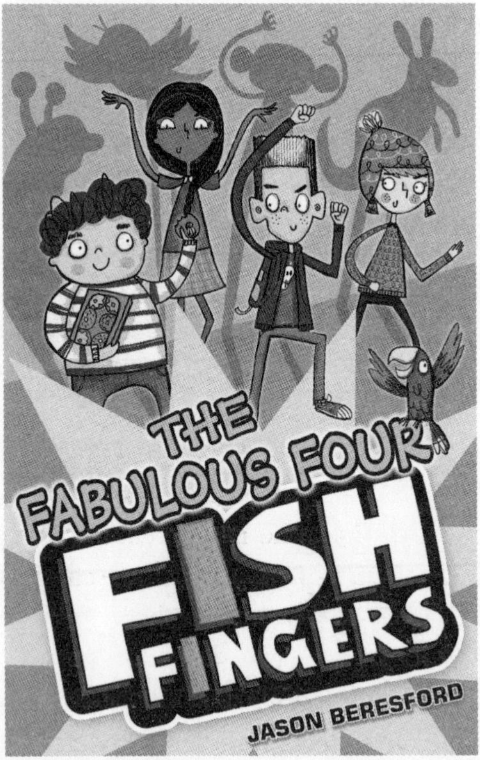

WARNING!!!!! This book contains a panteater. He will steal your sweets. And eat your pants.